A Floatin

Jules Gabriel Verne

Volume 8 of 54 in the

"Voyages Extraordinaires"

First published in 1871.

2012 Reprint by Kassock Bros. Publishing Co.

Printed in the United States Of America

Cover Illustration By Isaac M. Kassock

ISBN: 1478237139
ISBN-13: 978-1478237136

Jules Gabriel Verne (1828-1905)

The Extraordinary Voyages
of
Jules Verne
~

01 - Five Weeks in a Balloon
02 - The Adventures of Captain Hatteras
03 - Journey to the Center of the Earth
04 - From the Earth to the Moon
05 - In Search of the Castaways
06 - Twenty Thousand Leagues Under the Sea
07 - Around The Moon
08 - A Floating City
09 -The Adventures of Three Englishmen and Three Russians in South Africa
10 - The Fur Country
11 - Around the World in Eighty Days
12 - The Mysterious Island
13 - The Survivors of the *Chancellor*
14 - Michael Strogoff
15 - Off on a Comet
16 - The Child of the Cavern
17 – A Captain at Fifteen
18 - The Begum's Millions
19 - Tribulations of a Chinaman in China
20 - The Steam House
21 - Eight Hundred Leagues on the Amazon
22 - Godfrey Morgan
23 - The Green Ray
24 - Kéraban the Inflexible
25 - The Vanished Diamond
26 - The Archipelago on Fire
27 - Mathias Sandorf

28 - The Lottery Ticket
29 - Robur the Conqueror
30 - North Against South
31 - The Flight to France
32 - Two Years' Vacation
33 - Family Without a Name
34 - The Purchase of the North Pole
35 - César Cascabel
36 - Mistress Branican
37 - Carpathian Castle
38 - Claudius Bombarnac
39 - Foundling Mick
40 - Captain Antifer
41 - Propeller Island
42 - Facing the Flag
43 - Clovis Dardentor
44 - An Antarctic Mystery
45 - The Mighty Orinoco
46 - Will of an Eccentric
47 - The Castaways of the Flag
48 - The Village in the Treetops
49 - The Sea Serpent
50 - The Kip Brothers
51 - Traveling Scholarships
52 - A Drama in Livonia
53 - Master of the World
54 - Invasion of the Sea

Table of Contents

A FLOATING CITY

CHAPTER I

ON the 18th of March, 1867, I arrived at Liverpool, intending to take a berth simply as an amateur traveler on board the *Great Eastern,* which in a few days was to sail for New York. I had sometimes thought of paying a visit to North America, and was now tempted to cross the Atlantic on board this gigantic boat. First of all the *Great Eastern,* then the country celebrated by Cooper.

This steam-ship is indeed a masterpiece of naval construction; more than a vessel, it is a floating city, part of the country, detached from English soil, which after having crossed the sea, unites itself to the American Continent. I pictured to myself this enormous bulk borne on the waves, her defiant struggle with the wind, her boldness before the powerless sea, her indifference to the billows, her stability in the midst of that element which tosses " Warriors" and "Solferinos" like ship's boats. But my imagination carried me no farther; all these things I did indeed see during the passage, and many others which do not exclusively belong to the maritime domain. If the " Great Eastern" is not merely a nautical engine, but rather a microcosm, and carries a small world with it, an observer will not be astonished to meet here, as on a larger theater, all the instincts, follies, and passions of human nature.

On leaving the station, I went to the Adelphi Hotel. The *Great Eastern* was announced to sail on the 20th of March, and as I wished to witness the last preparations, I asked permission of Captain Anderson, the commander, to take my place on board immediately, which permission he very obligingly granted.

The next day I went down towards the basins which form a double line of docks on the banks of the Mersey. The gate-keepers allowed me to go on to Prince's Landing Stage, a kind of movable raft which rises and falls with the tide, and is a landing place for the numerous boats which run between Liverpool, and the opposite town of Birkenhead on the left bank of the Mersey.

The Mersey, like the Thames, is only an insignificant stream, unworthy the name of river, although it falls into the sea.

It is an immense depression of the land filled with water, in fact nothing more than a hole, the depth of which allows it to receive ships of the heaviest tonnage, such as the *Great Eastern*, to which almost every other port in the world is closed. Thanks to this natural condition, the streams of the Thames and the Mersey have seen two immense commercial cities, London and Liverpool, built almost at their mouths, and from a similar cause has Glasgow arisen on the Clyde.

At Prince's Landing-Stage, a small tug in the service of the *Great Eastern* was getting up steam. I went on board and found it already crowded with workmen and mechanics. As the clock in Victoria Tower struck seven, the tender left her moorings and quickly ascended the Mersey with the rising tide.

Scarcely had we started, when I saw on the quay a tall young man, with that aristocratic look which so distinguishes the English officer. I thought I recognized in him a friend whom I had not seen for several years, a captain in the Indian army; but I must have been mistaken, for Captain Mac Elwin could not have left Bombay, as I ought to have known, besides Mac Elwin was a gay, careless fellow, and a jovial companion, but this person, if lie resembled him in feature, seemed melancholy, and as though burdened with a secret grief. Be it as it may, I had not time to observe him more closely, for the tender was moving rapidly away, and the impression founded on this resemblance soon vanished from my mind.

The *Great Eastern* was anchored about three miles up the river, at a depth equal to the height of the tallest houses in Liverpool. She was not to be seen from Prince's Stage, but I caught a glimpse of her imposing bulk from the first bend in the river.

One would have taken her for a small island, hardly discernible in the mist. She appeared with her bows towards us, having swung round with the tide; but soon the tender altered her course, and the whole length of the steam-ship was presented to our view; she seemed what in fact she was-enormous! Three or four colliers alongside were pouring their cargoes of coal into her port-holes. Beside the *Great Eastern*, these three-mast ships looked like barges; their funnels did not even reach the first line of light-ports in her hull; the yards of their gallant- sails did not come up to her bulwarks. The giant could have hoisted these ships on its davits like shore-boats.

Meanwhile the tender approached the *Great Eastern,* whose chains were violently strained by the pressure of the tide, and ranged up to the foot of an immense winding staircase, on the port side. In this position the deck of the tender was only on a level with the load water-line of the steam-ship, to which line she would be depressed when in full cargo, and which still emerged two yards.

The workmen were now hurriedly disembarking and clambering up the numerous steps which terminated at the fore-part of the ship. I, with head upturned, and my body thrown back, surveyed the wheels of the *Great Eastern,* like a tourist looking up at a high edifice.

Seen from the side, these wheels looked narrow and contracted, although their paddles were four yards broad, but in front they had a monumental aspect. Their elegant fittings, the arrangements of the whole plan, the stays crossing each other to support the division of the triple center rim, the radius of red spokes, the machinery half lost in the shadow of the wide paddle-boxes, all this impressed the mind, and awakened an idea of some gigantic and mysterious power.

With what force must these wooden paddles strike the waves which are now gently breaking over them! What a boiling of water when this powerful engine strikes it blow after blow! What a thundering noise engulfed in this paddle-box cavern! When the *Great Eastern* goes at full speed, under the pressure of wheels measuring fifty-three feet in diameter and 166 in circumference, weighing ninety tons, and making eleven revolutions a minute. The tender had disembarked her crew; I stepped on to the fluted iron steps, and in a few minutes had crossed the fore-part of the *Great Eastern.*

CHAPTER II

THE deck was still nothing but an immense timber-yard given up to an army of workmen. I could not believe I was on board a ship. Several thousand men-workmen, crew, engineers, officers, mechanics, lookers-on-mingled and jostled together without the least concern, some on deck, others in the engine-room; here pacing the upper decks, there scattered in the rigging, all in an indescribable pell-mell. Here fly-wheel cranes were raising enormous pieces of cast-iron, there heavy joists were hoisted by steam windlasses; above the engine-rooms an iron cylinder, a metal shaft in fact, was balanced. At the bows, the yards creaked as the sails were hoisted; at the stern rose a scaffolding which, doubtless, concealed some building in construction. Building, fixing, carpentering, rigging, and painting, were going on in the midst of the greatest disorder.

My luggage was already on board. I asked to see Captain Anderson, and was told that he had not yet arrived; but one of the stewards undertook to install me, and had my packages carried to one of the aft cabins.

"My good fellow," said I to him, "the *Great Eastern* was announced to sail on the 2oth of March, but is it possible that we can be ready in twenty-four hours? Can you tell me when we may expect to leave Liverpool?"

But in this respect the steward knew no more than I did, and he left me to myself. I then made up my mind to visit all the ins and outs of this immense ant-hill, and began my walk like a tourist in a foreign town. A black mire-that British mud which is so rarely absent from the pavement of English towns-covered the deck of the steamship; dirty gutters wound here and there. One might have thought oneself in the worst part of Upper Thames Street, near London Bridge. I walked on, following the upper decks towards the stern. Stretching on either side were two wide streets, or rather boulevards, filled with a compact crowd; thus walking, I came to the center of the steam-ship between the paddles, united by a double set of bridges.

Here opened the pit containing the machinery of the paddle-wheels, and I had an opportunity of looking at this admirable locomotive engine. About fifty workmen were scattered on the metallic skylights, some clinging to the long suction-pumps fixing the eccentric wheels, others hanging on the cranks riveting iron wedges with enormous wrenches. After having cast a rapid glance over these fitting works, I continued my walk till I reached the bows, where the carpenters were finishing the decoration of a large saloon called the "smoking-room," a magnificent apartment with fourteen windows; the ceiling white and gold, and wainscoted with lemon-coloured panels. Then, after having crossed a small triangular space at the bows, I reached the stem, which descends perpendicularly into the water.

Turning round from this extreme point, through an opening in the mists, I saw the stern of the *Great Eastern* at a distance of more than two hundred yards.

I returned by the boulevards on the starboard side, avoiding contact with the swaying pulleys and the ropes of the rigging, lashed in all directions by the wind; now keeping out of the way, here of the blows of a fly-wheel crane, and further on, of the flaming scoria which were showering from a forge like a display of fireworks. I could hardly see the tops of the masts, two hundred feet in height, which lost themselves in the mist, increased by the black smoke from the tenders and colliers.

After having passed the great hatchway of the engine rooms, I observed a "small hotel" on my left, and then the spacious side walls of a palace surmounted by a terrace, the railings of which were being varnished. At last I reached the stern of the steam-ship, and the place I had already noticed where the scaffolding was erected. Here between the last small deck cabin and the enormous gratings of the hatchways, above which rose the four wheels of the rudder, some engineers had just finished placing a steam engine. The engine was composed of two horizontal cylinders, and presented a system of pinions, levers, and wheels which seemed to me very complicated. I did not understand at first for what it was intended, but it appeared that here, as everywhere else, the preparations were far from complete.

And now, why all these delays? Why so many new arrangements on board the *Great Eastern,* a comparatively new ship? The reason may be explained in a few words.

After twenty passages from England to America, one of which was marked by very serious disasters, the use of the *Great Eastern* was temporarily abandoned, and this immense ship, arranged to accommodate passengers, seemed no longer good for anything. When the first attempt to lay the Atlantic cable had failed, -partly because the number of ships which carried it was insufficient- engineers thought of the *Great Eastern.* She alone could store on board the 2100 miles of metallic wire, weighing 4500 tons. She alone, thanks to her perfect indifference to the sea, could unroll and immerse this immense cable. But special arrangements were necessary for storing away the cable in the ship's hold. Two out of six boilers were removed, and one funnel out of three belonging to the screw engine; in their places large tanks were placed for the cable, which was immersed in water to preserve it from the effects of variation of the atmosphere; the wire thus passed from these tanks of water into the sea without suffering the least contact with the air.

The laying of the cable having been successfully accomplished, and the object in view attained, the *Great Eastern* was once more left in her costly idleness. A French company, called the "Great Eastern Company, Limited," was floated with a capital of 2,000,000 francs, with the intention of employing the immense ship for the conveyance of passengers across the Atlantic. Thus the reason for rearranging the ship to this purpose, and the consequent necessity of filling up the tanks and replacing the boilers, of enlarging the saloons in which so many people were to live during the voyage, and of building extra dining saloons, finally the arrangement of a thousand berths in the sides of the gigantic hull

The *Great Eastern* was freighted to the amount of 25,000 francs a month. Two contracts were arranged with *G. Forrester and Co.,* of Liverpool, the first to the amount of 538,750 francs, for making new boilers for the screw; the second to the amount of 662,500 francs for general repairs, and fixings on board.

Before entering upon the last undertaking, the Board of Trade required that the ship's hull should undergo a strict examination. This costly operation accomplished, a long crack in her exterior plates was carefully repaired at a great expense, and the next proceeding was to fix the new boilers; the driving main-shaft of the wheels, which had been damaged during the last voyage, had to be replaced by a shaft, provided with two eccentric wheels, which insured the solidity of this important part. And now for the first time the *Great Eastern* was to be steered by steam. It was for this delicate operation that the engineers intended the engine which they had placed at the stern. The steersman standing on the bridge between the signal apparatus connected with the paddle-wheels and that connected with the screw, has before his eyes a dial provided with a moving needle, which tells him every moment the position of his rudder. In order to modify it, he has only to press his hand lightly on a small wheel, measuring hardly a foot in diameter, and placed within his reach. Immediately the valves open, the steam from the boilers rushes along the conducting tubes into the two cylinders of the small engine, the pistons move rapidly, and the rudder instantly obeys. If this plan succeeds, a man will be able to direct the gigantic body of the *Great Eastern* with one finger.

For five days operations continued with distracting activity. These delays considerably affected the enterprise of the freighters, but the contractors could do no more. The day for setting sail was irrevocably settled for the 26th of March. The 25th still saw the deck strewn with all kinds of tools.

During this last day, however, little by little the gangways were cleared, the scaffoldings were taken down, the fly-wheel cranes disappeared, the fixing of the engines was accomplished, the last screws and nails were driven in, the reservoirs filled with oil, and the last slab rested on its metal mortise. This day the chief engineer tried the boilers. The engine-rooms were full of steam; leaning over the hatchway, enveloped in a hot mist, I could see nothing, but I heard the long pistons groaning, and the huge cylinders noisily swaying to and fro on their solid swing blocks. The muddy waters of the Mersey were lashed into foam by the slowly revolving paddle- heels; at the stem, the screw beat the waves with its four blades; the two engines, entirely independent of each other, were in complete working order.

Towards five o'clock a small steamer, intended as a shore-boat for the *Great Eastern*, came alongside. Her movable engine was first hoisted on board by means of windlasses, but as for the steamer herself, she could not be embarked. Her steel hull was so heavy that the davits to which it was attached bent under the weight, undoubtedly this would not have occurred had they supported them with lifts. Therefore they were obliged to abandon the steamer, but there still remained on the *Great Eastern* a string of sixteen boats hanging to the davits.

Everything was finished by evening; not a trace of mud was visible on the well-swept boulevards, for an army of sweepers had been at work. There was a full cargo; provisions, goods, and coal filled the stewards' room, the store, and the coal houses. However, the steamer had not yet sunk to the load water-line, and did not draw the necessary thirty-three feet It was an inconvenient position for the wheels, for the paddles not being sufficiently immersed, caused a great diminution in the speed.

Nevertheless it was possible to set sail, and I went to bed with the hope of starting next day. I was not disappointed, for at break of dawn I saw the English, French, and American flags floating from the masts.

CHAPTER III

The *Great Eastern* was indeed preparing to sail. Already volumes of black smoke were issuing from the five chimneys, and hot steam filled the engine-rooms. Some sailors were brightening up the four great fog-cannons which were to salute Liverpool as we sailed by. The top-men climbed the yards, disentangled the rigging, and tightened the shrouds on the thick ropes fastened to the bulwarks. About eleven o'clock the carpenters and painters put the finishing touches to their work, and then embarked on board the tender which awaited them. As soon as there was a sufficient pressure, the steam rushed into the cylinders of the rudder engine, and the engineers had the pleasure of seeing that this ingenious contrivance was an entire success.

The weather was fine, with bright gleams of sunshine darting through the rapidly-moving clouds. There must have been a strong breeze at sea, but we did not feel it.

The officers were all dispersed about the deck, making preparations for getting under sail. The ship's officers were composed of the Captain, the first officer, two assistant officers, five lieutenants, of whom one was a Frenchman, M. H-, and a volunteer who was also French.

Captain Anderson holds a high place in the commercial marine of England. It is to him we are indebted for the laying of the Transatlantic cable, though it is true that if he succeeded where his predecessors had failed, it was because he worked under more favorable circumstances, having the *Great Eastern* at his command. Be it as it may, his success gained for him the title of "Sir." I found him to be a very agreeable commander. He was a man of about fifty years of age, with that tawny complexion which remains unchanged by weather or age; a thorough Englishman, with a tall figure, a broad smiling face, and merry eyes; walking with a quiet dignified step, his hands never in his pockets, always irreproachably gloved and elegantly dressed, and invariably with a little piece of his white handkerchief peeping out of the pocket of his blue and gold-laced overcoat.

The first officer presented a singular contrast to Captain Anderson, and his appearance is easily described: an active little man, with a very sunburnt skin, a black beard almost covering his face, and legs which defied every lurch of the vessel A skillful, energetic seaman, he gave his orders in a clear, decided tone, the boatswain repeating them with a voice like the roaring of a hoarse lion. The second officer's name was W--: I think he was a naval officer, on board the *Great Eastern* by special permission; he had all the appearance of a regular "Jack-tar."

Besides the ship officers, the engines were under the command of a chief engineer, assisted by eight or ten engineering officers, and a battalion of two hundred and fifty men, some stokers, others oilers, who hardly ever left the engine-rooms.

This army of men was well occupied night and day, having ten boilers with ten furnaces and about a hundred fires to attend to.

As for the crew of the steam-ship proper, what with quartermasters, topmen, gearmen, and cabin-boys, it comprised about one hundred men, and besides these, there were two hundred stewards employed for waiting on the passengers.

Every man was at his post; the pilot who was to conduct the vessel out of the Mersey had been on board since the evening before. I saw also a French pilot, who was to make the passage with us, and on her return to take the steam-ship into anchorage at Brest.

"I begin to think we shall sail today," said I to Lieutenant

H--.

"We are only waiting for our passengers," replied my countryman.

"Are there many?"

"Twelve or thirteen hundred."

At half-past eleven the tender was hailed, laden with passengers, who, as I afterwards learnt, were Californians, Canadians, Americans, Peruvians, English, Germans, and two or three Frenchmen. Among the most distinguished were the celebrated Cyrus Field of New York, the Honourable John Rose of Canada, the Honourable J. Mac Alpine of New York, Mr. and Mrs. Alfred Cohen of San Francisco, Mr. and Mrs. Whitney of Montreal, Captain Mc Ph-- and his wife. Among the French was the founder of the "Great Eastern Freight Company," M. Jules D--, representative of the " Telegraph Construction and Maintenance Company," who had made a contribution of twenty thousand pounds to the fund.

The tender ranged herself at the foot of a flight of steps, and then began the slow, interminable ascent of passengers and luggage. The first care of each passenger, when he had once set foot on the steamer, was to go and secure his place in the dining-room; his card, or his name written on a scrap of paper, was enough to insure his possession.

I remained on deck in order to notice all the details of embarkation. At half-past twelve the luggage was all on board, and I saw thousands of packages of every description, from chests large enough to contain a suite of furniture, to elegant little travelling-cases and fanciful American and English trunks, heaped together pell-mell. All these were soon cleared from the deck, and stowed away in the store-rooms; workmen and porters returned to the tender, which steered off, after having blackened the side of the *Great Eastern* with her smoke.

I was going back towards the bows, when suddenly I found myself face to face with the young man I had seen on Prince's Landing-Stage. He stopped on seeing me, and held out his hand, which I warmly shook.

"You, Fabian!" I cried. "You here?"

"Even so, my dear friend."

“I was not mistaken, then; it was really you I saw on the quay a day or two since.”

"It is most likely," replied Fabian, "but I did not see you."

“And you are going to America?”

"Certainly! Do you think I could spend a month's leave better than in traveling?"

"How fortunate that you thought of making your tour in the *Great Eastern*!"

"It was not chance at all, my dear fellow. I read in the newspaper that you were one of the passengers; and as we have not met for some years now, I came on board in order to make the passage with you."

“Have you come from India?"

“Yes, by the *Godavery*, which arrived at Liverpool the day before yesterday."

"And you are traveling, Fabian?" I asked, noticing his pale, sad face.

"To divert my mind, if I can," interrupted Captain Mac Elwin, warmly pressing my hand.

CHAPTER IV

Fabian left me, to look for his cabin, which, according to the ticket he held in his hand, was number seventy-three of the grand saloon series. At this moment large volumes of smoke curled from the chimneys; the steam hissed with a deafening noise through the escape-pipes, and fell in a fine rain over the deck; a noisy eddying of water announced that the engines were at work. We were at last going to start.

First of all the anchor had to be raised. The *Great Eastern* swung round with the tide; all was now clear, and Captain Anderson was obliged to choose this moment to set sail, for the width of the *Great Eastern* did not allow of her turning round in the Mersey. He was more master of his ship and more certain of guiding her skillfully in the midst of the numerous boats always plying on the river when stemming the rapid current than when driven by the ebb-tide; the least collision with this gigantic body would have proved disastrous.

To weigh anchor under these circumstances required considerable exertion, for the pressure of the tide stretched the chains by which the ship was moored, and besides this, a strong south-wester blew with full force on her hull, so that it required powerful engines to hoist the heavy anchors from their muddy beds. An anchor-boat, intended for this purpose, had just stoppered on the chains, but the windlasses were not sufficiently powerful, and they were obliged to use the steam apparatus which the *Great Eastern* had at her disposal.

At the bows was an engine of sixty-six horse-power. In order to raise the anchors it was only necessary to send the steam from the boilers into its cylinders to obtain immediately a considerable power, which could be directly applied to the windlass on which the chains were fastened. This was done; but powerful as it was, this engine was found insufficient, and fifty of the crew were set to turn the capstan with bars, thus the anchors were gradually drawn in, but it was slow work.

I was on the top-gallant forecastle with several other passengers at this moment, watching the details of departure. Near me stood a traveler, who frequently shrugged his shoulders impatiently, and did not spare disparaging jokes on the tardiness of the work. He was a thin, nervous little man, with quick, restless eyes: a physiognomist could easily see that the things of this life always appeared on their funny side to this philosopher of Democrates school, for his risible muscles were never still for a moment; but without describing him further, I need only say I found him a very pleasant fellow-traveler

"I thought until now, sir," said he to me, " that engines were made to help men, not men to help engines."

I was going to reply to this wise observation, when there was a loud cry, and immediately my companion and I were hurled towards the bows; every man at the capstan-bars was knocked down; some got up again, others lay scattered on the deck. A catch had broken, and the capstan being forced round by the frightful pressure of the chains, the men, caught by the rebound, were struck violently on the head and chest freed from their broken rope-bands, the capstan-bars flew in all directions like grape-shot, killing four sailors, and wounding twelve others; among the latter was the boatswain, a Scotchman from Dundee.

The spectators hurried towards the unfortunate men, the wounded were taken to the hospital at the stern; as for the four already dead, preparations were immediately made to send them on shore: so lightly do Anglo-Saxons regard death, that this event made very little impression on board. These unhappy men, killed and wounded, were only tools, which could be replaced at very little expense. The tender, already some distance off, was hailed, and in a few minutes she was alongside.

I went towards the fore-part of the vessel, the staircase had not yet been raised. The four corpses, enveloped in coverings, were let down, and placed on the deck of the tender. One of the surgeons on board embarked to go with them to Liverpool, with injunctions to rejoin the *Great Eastern* as quickly as possible. The tender immediately sheered off, and the sailors went to the bows, to wash the stains of blood from the deck.

I ought to add that one of the passengers, slightly wounded by the breaking of the pinion, took advantage of this circumstance to leave by the tender; he had already had enough of the *Great Eastern*.

I watched the little boat going off full steam, and, turning round, I heard my ironical fellow-traveler mutter,

“A good beginning for a voyage!”

"A very bad one, sir," said I. "To whom have I the honour of speaking?"

"To Dr. Dean Pitferge."

CHAPTER V

The work of weighing anchors was resumed; with the help of the anchor-boat the chains were eased, and the anchors at last left their tenacious depths. A quarter past one sounded from the Birkenhead clock-towers, the moment of departure could not be deferred, if it was intended to make use of the tide. The captain and pilot went on the foot-bridge; one lieutenant placed himself near the screw-signal apparatus, another near that of the paddle-wheel, in case of the failure of the steam-engine; four other steersmen watched at the stern, ready to put in action the great wheels placed on the gratings of the hatchings. The *Great Eastern,* making head against the current, was now only waiting to descend the river with the ebb-tide.

The order for departure was given, the paddles slowly struck the water, the screw bubbled at the stern, and the enormous vessel began to move.

The greater part of the passengers on the poop were gazing at the double landscape of Liverpool and Birkenhead, studded with manufactory chimneys. The Mersey, covered with ships, some lying at anchor, others ascending and descending the river, offered only a winding passage for our steam-ship. But under the hand of a pilot, sensible to the least inclinations of her rudder, she glided through the narrow passages, like a whale-boat beneath the oar of a vigorous steersman. At one time I thought that we were going to run foul of a brig, which was drifting across the stream, her bows nearly grazing the hull of the *Great Eastern*, but a collision was avoided, and when from the height of the upper deck I looked at this ship, which was not of less than seven or eight hundred tons burden, she seemed to me no larger than the tiny boats which children play with on the lakes of Regent's Park or the Serpentine. It was not long before the *Great Eastern* was opposite the Liverpool landing-stages, but the four cannons which were to have saluted the town, were silent out of respect to the dead, for the tender was disembarking them at this moment; however, loud hurrahs replaced the reports which are the last expressions of national politeness. Immediately there was a vigorous clapping of hands and waving of handkerchiefs, with all the enthusiasm with which the English hail the departure of every vessel, be it only a simple yacht sailing round a bay. But with what shouts they were answered! What echoes they called forth from the quays! There were thousands of spectators on both the Liverpool and Birkenhead sides, and boats laden with sight-seers swarmed on the Mersey. The sailors manning the yards of the *Lord Clyde*, lying at anchor opposite the docks, saluted the giant with their hearty cheers.

But even the noise of the cheering could not drown the frightful discord of several bands playing at the same time. Flags were incessantly hoisted in honour of the *Great Eastern,* but soon the cries grew faint in the distance. Our steam-ship ranged near the *Tripoli*, a Cunard emigrant-boat, which in spite of her 2000 tons burden looked like a mere barge; then the houses grew fewer and more scattered on both shores, the landscape was no longer blackened with smoke; and brick walls, with the exception of some long regular buildings intended for workmen's houses, gave way to the open country, with pretty villas dotted here and there. Our last salutation reached us from the platform of the lighthouse and the walls of the bastion.

At three o'clock the *Great Eastern* had crossed the bar of the Mersey, and shaped her course down St George's Channel There was a strong sou'wester blowing, and a heavy swell on the sea, but the steamship did not feel it

Towards four o'clock the Captain gave orders to heave to; the tender put on full steam to rejoin us, as she was bringing back the doctor. When the boat came alongside a rope-ladder was thrown out, by which he ascended, not without some difficulty. Our more agile pilot slid down by the same way into his boat, which was awaiting him, each rower provided with a cork jacket. Some minutes after he went on board a charming little schooner waiting to catch the breeze.

Our course was immediately continued; under the pressure of the paddles and the screw, the speed of the *Great Eastern* greatly increased; in spite of the wind ahead, she neither rolled nor pitched. Soon the shades of night stretched across the sea, and Holyhead Point was lost in the darkness.

CHAPTER VI

The next day, the 27th of March, the *Great Eastern* coasted along the deeply-indented Irish shore. I had chosen my cabin at the bows; it was a small room well lighted by two skylights. A second row of cabins separated it from the first saloon, so that neither the noise of conversation, nor the rattling of pianos, which were not wanting on board, could reach me. It was an isolated cabin; the furniture consisted of a sofa, a bedstead, and a toilet-table.

The next morning at seven o'clock, having crossed the first two rooms, I went on deck. A few passengers were already pacing the upper decks; an almost imperceptible swell rocked the steamer; the wind, however, was high, but the sea, protected by the coast, was comparatively calm.

From the poop of the smoking-room, I perceived that long line of shore, the continual verdure of which has won for it the name of " Emerald Coast." A few solitary houses, a string of tide waiters, a wreath of white smoke curling from between two hills, indicating the passing of a train, an isolated signal-post making grimacing gestures to the vessels at large, here and there animated the scene.

The sea between us and the coast was of a dull green shade; there was a fresh breeze blowing, mists floated above the water like spray. Numerous vessels, brigs and schooners, were awaiting the tide; steamers puffing away their black smoke were soon distanced by the *Great Eastern*, although she was going at a very moderate speed.

Soon we came in sight of Queenstown, a small "callingplace," before which several fishermen's boats were at work. It is here that all ships bound for Liverpool, whether steamers or sailing-ships, throw out their dispatch-bags, which are carried to Dublin in a few hours by an express train always in readiness. From Dublin they are conveyed across the channel to Holyhead by a fast steamer, so that dispatches thus sent are one day in advance of the most rapid Transatlantic steamers.

About nine o'clock the course of the *Great Eastern* was west-north-west. I was just going on deck, when I met Captain Mac Elwin, accompanied by a friend, a tall, robust man, with a light beard and long mustache which mingled with the whiskers and left the chin bare, after the fashion of the day. This tall fellow was the exact type of an English officer; his figure was erect without stiffness, his look calm, his walk dignified but easy; his whole appearance seemed to indicate unusual courage, and I was not mistaken in him.

"My friend, Archibald Corsican," said Fabian to me, "a captain in the 22nd regiment of the Indian army, like myself."

Thus introduced, Captain Corsican and I bowed.

"We hardly saw each other yesterday, Fabian," said I, shaking Captain Mac Elwin's hand, "we were in the bustle of departure, so that all I know about you is that it was not chance which brought you on board the *Great*

Eastern. I must confess that if I have anything to do with your decision-"

"Undoubtedly, my dear fellow," interrupted Fabian; "Captain Corsican and I came to Liverpool with the intention of taking our berths on board the *China*, a Cunard steamer, when we heard that the *Great Eastern* was going to attempt another passage from England to America; it was a chance we might not get again, and learning that you were on board I did not hesitate, as I had not seen you since we took that delightful trip in the Scandinavian States three years ago; so now you know how it was that the tender brought us here yesterday."

"My dear Fabian," I replied, "I believe that neither Captain Corsican nor yourself will regret your decision, as a passage across the Atlantic in this huge boat cannot fail to be interesting even to you who are so little used to the sea. But now let us talk about yourself. Your last letter, and it is not more than six weeks since I received it, bore the Bombay post-mark, so that I was justified in believing you were still with your regiment."

"We were so three weeks ago," said Fabian, "leading the half-military, half-country life of Indian officers, employing most of our time in hunting; my friend here is a famed tiger-killer; however, as we are both single and without family ties, we thought we would let the poor wild beasts of the peninsula rest for a time, while we came to Europe to breathe a little of our native air. We obtained a year's leave, and traveling by way of the Red Sea, Suez, and France, we reached Old England with the utmost possible speed."

"Old England," said Captain Corsican, smiling; "we are there no longer, Fabian; we are on board an English ship, but it is freighted by a French company, and it is taking us to America; three different flags float over our heads, signifying that we are treading on Franco-Anglo-American boards."

"What does it matter," replied Fabian, and a painful expression passed over his face; "what does it matter, so long as it whiles away the time? 'Movement is life;' and it is well to be able to forget the past, and kill the present by continual change. In a few days I shall be at New York, where I hope to meet again my sister and her children, whom I have not seen for several years; then we shall visit the great lakes, and descend the Mississippi as far as New Orleans, where we shall look for sport on the Amazon. From America we are going to Africa, where the lions and elephants will make the Cape their 'rendezvous,' in order to celebrate the arrival of Captain Corsican. Finally, we shall return and impose on the Sepoys the caprices of the metropolis."

Fabian spoke with a nervous volubility, and his breast heaved; evidently there was some great grief weighing on his mind, the cause of which I was as yet ignorant of, but with which Archibald seemed to be well acquainted. He evinced a warm friendship for Fabian, who was several years younger than himself, treating him like a younger brother, with a devotion which at times almost amounted to heroism.

At this moment our conversation was interrupted by the sound of a horn, which announced the half-past twelve lunch. Four times a day, to the great satisfaction of the passengers, this shrill horn sounded: at half-past eight for breakfast, half-past twelve for lunch, four o'clock for dinner, and at seven for tea. In a few minutes the long streets were deserted, and soon the tables in the immense saloons were filled with guests. I succeeded in getting a place near Fabian and Captain Corsican.

The dining-rooms were provided with four long rows of tables; the glasses and bottles placed in swing-racks kept perfectly steady; the roll of the steamer was almost imperceptible, so that the guests-men, women, and children-could eat their lunch without any fear. Numerous waiters were busy carrying round the tastily-arranged dishes, and supplying the demands for wine and beer; the Californians certainly distinguished themselves by their proclivities for champagne. Near her husband sat an old laundress, who had found gold in the San Francisco washing-tubs, emptying a bottle of champagne in no time; two or three pale, delicate looking young ladies were eagerly devouring slices of red beef; and others discussing with evident satisfaction the merits of rhubarb tart, &c. Every one worked away in the highest spirits; one could have fancied oneself at a restaurant in the middle of Paris instead of the open sea.

Lunch over, the decks were again filled; people bowed and spoke to each other in passing as formally as if they were walking in Hyde Park; children played and ran about, throwing their balls and bowling hoops as they might have done on the gravel walks of the Tuileries; the greater part of the men walked up and down smoking; the ladies, seated on folding-chairs, worked, read, or talked together, whilst the governesses and nurses looked after the children. A few corpulent Americans swung themselves backwards and forwards in their rocking-chairs; the ship's officers were continually passing to and fro, some going to their watch on the bridge, others answering the absurd questions put to them by some of the passengers; whilst the tones of an organ and two or three pianos making a distracting discord, reached us through the lulls in the wind.

About three o'clock a loud shouting was heard; the passengers crowded on to the poop; the *Great Eastern* had ranged within two cable-lengths of a vessel which she had overhauled. It was the *Propontis*, on her way to New York, saluting the giant of the seas on her passage, which compliment the giant returned.

Land was still in sight at four o'clock, but hardly discernible through the mist which had suddenly surrounded us. Soon we saw the light of Fastenet Beacon, situated on an isolated rock. Night set in, during which we must have doubled Cape Clear, the most southerly point of Ireland.

CHAPTER VII

I said that the length of the *Great Eastern* exceeded two hectometres. For the benefit of those partial to comparisons, I will add that it is a third longer than the *Pont des Arts*; in reality this steam-ship measures 673 feet at the load water-line, between the perpendiculars; the upper deck is 680 feet from stem to stern; that is to say, its length is double that of the largest transatlantic steamers, its width amidships is about 71 feet, and behind the paddles about 107 feet.

The hull of the *Great Eastern* is proof against the most formidable seas; it is double, and is composed of a number of cells placed between the deck and hold; besides these, thirteen compartments, separated by water-tight partitions, increase the security against fire or the inlet of water. Ten thousand tons of iron were used in the construction of this hull, and 3,000,000 rivets secured the iron plates on her sides.

The *Great Eastern* draws 30 feet of water with a cargo of 28,500 tons, and with a light cargo, from 20 to 30 feet She is capable of receiving 10,000 passengers, so that out of the 373 principal districts in France, 274 are less populated than this floating sub-prefecture with its average number of passengers.

The lines of the *Great Eastern* are very elongated; her straight stem is pierced, with hawse-holes, through which the anchor-chains pass; no signs of dents or protuberances are to be seen on her finely-cut bows, but the slight sweep of her rounded stem somewhat mars the general effect.

From the deck rise six masts and five funnels. The three masts in front are the "jigger," and the "fore-mast," and the " main-mast." The last three astern are the "after-main-mast," " mizen-mast," and "after-jigger." The fore-masts and the main-masts carry the schooner-sails, the top-sails, and the gallant-sails; the four other masts are only rigged with ordinary sails; the whole forming 5400 square yards of good canvas. On the spacious mast-tops of the second and third masts a band of soldiers could easily maneuver. Of these six masts, supported by shrouds and metallic back- stays, the second, third, and fourth are made of sheet iron, and are really masterpieces of ironwork. At the base they measure 43 inches in diameter, and the largest (the main-mast) rises to the height of 207 French feet, which is higher than the towers of Notre Dame.

As to the chimneys, the two belonging to the paddle engine and the three belonging to the screw, they are enormous cylinders, 90 feet high, supported by chains fastened to the upper deck. The arrangements with regard to the interior are admirable. The laundries and the crew's berths are shut off at the fore-part, then come the ladies' saloon and a grand saloon ornamented with lustres, swinging lamps, and pictures. These magnificent rooms are lighted by side sky-lights, supported on elegant-gilded pillars, and communicate with the upper-deck by wide staircases with metallic steps and mahogany balusters.

On deck are arranged four rows of cabins separated by a passage, some are reached by a landing, others on a lower story by private staircases. At the stern the three immense dining-rooms run in the same direction as the cabins, a passage leads from the saloons at the stern to those at the bows round the paddle-engine, between its sheet-iron partitions and the ship's offices.

The engines of the *Great Eastern* are justly considered as masterpieces-I was going to say of clockwork, for there is nothing more astonishing than to see this enormous machine working with the precision and ease of a clock, a singular contrast to the screw, which works rapidly and furiously, as though getting itself into a rage.

Independently of these two engines, the *Great Eastern* possesses six auxiliary ones to work the capstans, so that it is evident steam plays an important part on board. Such is this steam-ship, without equal and known everywhere; which, however, did not hinder a French captain from making this *naive* remark in his log-book: "Passed a ship with six masts and five chimneys, supposed to be the *Great Eastern*."

CHAPTER VIII

On Wednesday night the weather was very bad, my balance was strangely variable, and I was obliged to lean with my knees and elbows against the sideboard, to prevent myself from falling. Portmanteaus and bags came in and out of my cabin; an unusual hubbub reigned in the adjoining saloon, in which two or three hundred packages were making expeditions from one end to the other, knocking the tables and chairs with loud crashes; doors slammed, the boards creaked, the partitions made that groaning noise peculiar to pine wood; bottles and glasses jingled together in their racks, and a cataract of plates and dishes rolled about on the pantry floors. I heard the irregular roaring of the screw, and the wheels beating the water, sometimes entirely immersed, and at others striking the empty air; by all these signs I concluded that the wind had freshened, and the steam-ship was no longer indifferent to the billows.

At six o'clock next morning, after passing a sleepless night, I got up and dressed myself, as well as I could with one hand, while with the other I clutched at the sides of my cabin, for without support it was impossible to keep one's feet, and I had quite a serious struggle to get on my overcoat. I left my cabin, and helping myself with hands and feet through the billows of luggage, I crossed the saloon, scrambling up the stairs on my knees, like a Roman peasant devoutly climbing the steps of the *Scala Santa* of Pontius Pilate; and at last, reaching the deck, I hung on firmly to the nearest kevel.

No land in sight; we had doubled Cape Clear in the night, and around us was that vast circumference bounded by the line, where water and sky appear to meet the slate-coloured sea broke in great foamless billows. The *Great Eastern* struck amidships, and, supported by no sail, rolled frightfully, her bare masts describing immense circles in the air. There was no heaving to speak of, but the rolling was dreadful, it was impossible to stand upright. The officer on watch, clinging to the bridge, looked as if he was in a swing.

From stanchion to stanchion, I managed to reach the paddles on the starboard side, the deck was damp and slippery from the spray and mist: I was just going to fasten myself to a stanchion of the bridge when a body rolled at my feet. It was Dr. Pitferge, my quaint friend: he scrambled on to his knees, and looking at me, said,-

“That's all right, the amplitude of the arc, described by the sides of the *Great Eastern*, is forty degrees; that is, twenty degrees below the horizontal, and twenty above it."

“Indeed!” cried I, laughing, not at the observation, but at the circumstances under which it was made.

"Yes!" replied the Doctor. “During the oscillation the speed of the sides is fifty-nine inches per second, a transatlantic boat half the size takes but the same time to recover her equilibrium."

"Then," replied I, "since that is the case, there is an excess of stability in the *Great Eastern*.”

"For her, yes, but not for her passengers,” answered Dean Pitferge gaily, "for you see they come back to the horizontal quicker than they care for."

The Doctor, delighted with his repartee, raised himself, and holding each other up, we managed to reach a seat on the poop. Dean Pitferge had come off very well, with only a few bruises, and I congratulated him on his lucky escape, as he might have broken his neck.

"Oh, it is not over yet," said he; "there is more trouble coming."

"To us?"

"To the steamer, and consequently to me, to us, and to all the passengers."

"If you are speaking seriously, why did you come on board!"

"To see what is going to happen, for I should not be at all ill-pleased to witness a shipwreck!" replied the Doctor, looking at me knowingly.

"Is this the first time you have been on board the *Great Eastern*?"

"No, I have already made several voyages in her, to satisfy my curiosity."

"You must not complain, then."

"I do not complain; I merely state facts, and patiently await the hour of the catastrophe."

Was the Doctor making fun of me? I did not know what to think, his small twinkling eyes looked very roguish; but I thought I would try him further.

"Doctor," I said, "I do not know on what facts your painful prognostics are founded, but allow me to remind you that the *Great Eastern* has crossed the Atlantic twenty times, and most of her passages have been satisfactory."

"That's of no consequence; this ship is bewitched, to use a common expression, she cannot escape her fate; I know it, and therefore have no confidence in her. Remember what difficulties the engineers had to launch her; I believe even that Brunel, who built her, died from the 'effects of the operation,' as we doctors say."

"Ah, Doctor," said I; "are you inclined to be materialist?"

"Why ask me that question?"

"Because I have noticed that many who do not believe in God believe in everything else, even in the evil eye."

"Make fun if you like, sir," replied the Doctor, "but allow me to continue my argument. The *Great Eastern* has already ruined several companies. Built for the purpose of carrying emigrants to Australia, she has never once been there; intended to surpass the ocean steamers in speed, she even remains inferior to them."

"From this," said I, "it is to be concluded that-"

"Listen a minute," interrupted the Doctor. "Already one of her captains has been drowned, and he one of the most skillful, for he knew how to prevent this rolling by keeping the ship a little ahead of the waves."

"Ah, well!" said I, "the death of that able man is to be regretted."

"Then," continued Dean Pitferge, without noticing my incredulity, "strange stories are told about this ship; they say that a passenger who lost his way in the hold of the ship, like a pioneer in the forests of America, has never yet been found."

"Ah!" exclaimed I ironically, "there's a fact!"

"They say, also, that during the construction of the boilers an engineer was melted by mistake in the steam-box."

" Bravo!" cried I; "the melted engineer! '*È ben trovato*.' Do you believe it, Doctor?"

"I believe," replied Pitferge, "I believe quite seriously that our voyage began badly, and that it will end in the same manner."

"But the *Great Eastern* is a solid structure," I said, "and built so firmly that she is able to resist the most furious seas like a solid block."

"Solid she is, undoubtedly," resumed the doctor; " but let her fall into the hollow of the waves, and see if she will rise again. Maybe she is a giant, but a giant whose strength is not in proportion to her size; her engines are too feeble for her. Have you ever heard speak of her nineteenth passage from Liverpool to New York?"

"No, Doctor."

"Well, I was on board. We left Liverpool on a Tuesday, the 10th of December; there were numerous passengers, and all full of confidence. Everything went well so long as we were protected by the Irish coast from the billows of the open sea; no rolling, no sea-sickness; the next day, even, the same stability; the passengers were delighted. On the 12th, however, the wind freshened towards morning; the Great Eastern, heading the waves, rolled considerably; the passengers, men and women, disappeared into the cabins. At four o'clock the wind blew a hurricane; the furniture began to dance; a mirror in the saloon was broken by a blow from the head of your humble servant; all the crockery was smashed to atoms; there was a frightful uproar; eight shore-boats were torn from the davits in one swoop. At this moment our situation was serious; the paddle-wheel-engine had to be stopped; an enormous piece of lead, displaced by a lurch of the vessel, threatened to fall into its machinery; however, the screw continued to send us on. Soon the wheels began turning again, but very slowly; one of them had been damaged during the stoppage, and its spokes and paddles scraped the hull of the ship. The engine had to be stopped again, and we had to content ourselves with the screw. The night was fearful; the fury of the tempest was redoubled; the Great Eastern had fallen into the trough of the sea and could not right herself; at break of day there was not a piece of iron-work remaining on the wheels. They hoisted a few sails in order to right the ship, but no sooner were they hoisted than they were carried away; confusion reigned everywhere; the cable-chains, torn from their beds, rolled from one side of the ship to the other; a cattle-pen was knocked in, and a cow fell into the ladies' saloon through the hatchway; another misfortune was the breaking of the rudder-chock, so that steering was no longer possible.

Frightful crashes were heard; an oil tank, weighing over three tons, had broken from its fixings, and, rolling across the tween-decks, struck the sides alternately like a battering-ram. Saturday passed in the midst of a general terror, the ship in the trough of the sea all the time. Not until Sunday did the wind begin to abate, an American engineer on board then succeeded in fastening the chains on the rudder; we turned little by little, and the Great Eastern righted herself. A week after we left Liverpool we reached Queenstown. Now, who knows, sir, where we shall be in a week?"

CHAPTER IX

It must be confessed the Doctor's words were not very comforting, the passengers would not have heard them without shuddering. Was he joking, or did he speak seriously? Was it, indeed true, that he went with the *Great Eastern* in all her voyages, to be present at some catastrophe? Everything is possible for an eccentric, especially when he is English.

However, the *Great Eastern* continued her course, tossing like a canoe, and keeping strictly to the loxodromic line of steamers. It is well known, that on a flat surface, the nearest way from one point to another is by a straight line. On a sphere it is the curved line formed by the circumference of great circles. Ships have an interest in following this route, in order to make the shortest passage, but sailing vessels cannot pursue this track against a head-wind; so that steamers alone are able to maintain a direct course, and take the route of the great circles. This is what the *Great Eastern* did, making a little for the north-west.

The rolling never ceased, that horrible sea-sickness; at the same time contagious and epidemic, made rapid progress. Several of the passengers, with wan, pallid faces, and sunken cheeks, remained on deck, in order to breathe the fresh air, the greater part of them were furious at the unlucky steam-ship, which was conducting herself like a mere buoy, and at the freighter's advertisements, which had stated that sea-sickness was "unknown on board."

At nine o'clock in the morning an object three or four miles off was signaled from the larboard quarter. Was it a waif, the carcass of a whale, or the hull of a ship? As yet it was not distinguishable. A group of convalescent passengers stood on the upper-deck, at the bows, looking at this waif which was floating three hundred miles from the nearest land.

Meanwhile the *Great Eastern* was bearing towards the object signaled; all opera-glasses were promptly raised, and there was no lack of conjecture. Between the Americans, and English, to whom every pretext for a wager is welcome, betting at once commenced. Among the most desperate of the betters I noticed a tall man, whose countenance struck me as one of profound duplicity. His features were stamped with a look of general hatred, which neither a physiognomist, nor physiologist could mistake; his forehead was seamed with a deep furrow, his manner was at the same time audacious and listless, his eyebrows nearly meeting, partly concealed the stony eyes beneath, his shoulders were high and his chin thrust forward, in fact all the indications of insolence and knavery were united in his appearance. He spoke in loud pompous tones, while some of his worthy associates laughed at his coarse jokes. This personage pretended to recognize in the waif the carcass of a whale, and he backed his opinion by heavy stakes, which soon found ready acceptance.

These wagers, amounting to several hundred dollars, he lost every one; in fact, the waif was the hull of a ship; the steamer rapidly drew near it, and we could already see the rusty copper of her keel. It was a three-mast ship of about five or six hundred tons, deprived of her masts and rigging, and lying on one side, with broken chains hanging from her davits.

" Had this steam-ship been abandoned by her crew?" This was now the prevailing question, however no one appeared on the deck, perhaps the shipwrecked ones had taken refuge inside. I saw an object moving for several moments at the bows, but it turned out to be only the remains of the jib lashed to and fro by the wind. The hull was quite visible at the distance of half a mile; she was a comparatively new ship, and in a perfect state of preservation; her cargo, which had been shifted by the wind, obliged her to lie along on her starboard side.

The *Great Eastern* drew nearer, and, passing round, gave notice of her presence by several shrill whistles; but the waif remained silent, and unanimated; nothing was to be seen, not even a shore-boat from the wrecked vessel was visible on the wide expanse of water.

The crew had undoubtedly had time to leave her, but could they have reached land, which was three hundred miles off? Could a frail boat live on a sea like that which had rocked the *Great Eastern* so frightfully? And when could this catastrophe have happened? It was evident that the shipwreck had taken place farther west, for the wind and waves must have driven the hull far out of her course. These questions were destined to remain unanswered.

When the steam-ship came alongside the stern of the wreck, I could read distinctly the name *Lerida*, but the port she belonged to was not given. A merchant-vessel or a man-of-war would have had no hesitation in manning this hull which, undoubtedly, contained a valuable cargo, but as the *Great Eastern* was on regular service, she could not take this waif in tow for so many hundreds of miles; it was equally impossible to return and take it to the nearest port. Therefore, to the great regret of the sailors, it had to be abandoned, and it was soon a mere speck in the distance. The group of passengers dispersed, some to the saloons, others to their cabins, and even the lunch-bell failed to awaken the slumberers, worn out by sea-sickness. About noon Captain Anderson ordered sail to be hoisted, so that the ship, better supported, did not roll so much.

CHAPTER X

In spite of the ship's disorderly conduct, life on board was becoming organized, for with the Anglo Saxon nothing is more simple. The steam-boat is his street and his house for the time being; the Frenchman, on the contrary, always looks like a traveler

When the weather was favorable, the boulevards were thronged with promenaders, who managed to maintain the perpendicular, in spite of the ship's motion, but with the peculiar gyrations of tipsy men. When the passengers did not go on deck, they remained either in their private sitting-rooms or in the grand saloon, and then began the noisy discords of pianos, all played at the same time, which, however, seemed not to affect Saxon ears in the least. Among these amateurs, I noticed a tall, bony woman, who must have been a good musician, for, in order to facilitate reading her piece of music, she had marked all the notes with a number, and the piano-keys with a number corresponding, so that if it was note twenty-seven, she struck key twenty-seven, if fifty-three, key fifty-three, and so on, perfectly indifferent to the noise around her, or the sound of other pianos in the adjoining saloons, and her equanimity was not even disturbed when some disagreeable little children thumped with their fists on the unoccupied keys.

Whilst this concert was going on, a bystander would carelessly take up one of the books scattered here and there on the tables, and, having found an interesting passage, would read it aloud, whilst his audience listened good-humouredly, and complimented him with a flattering murmur of applause. Newspapers were scattered on the sofas, generally American and English, which always look old, although the pages have never been cut; it is a very tiresome operation reading these great sheets, which take up so much room, but the fashion being to leave them uncut, so they remain. One day I had the patience to read the *New York Herald* from beginning to end under these circumstances, and judge if I was rewarded for my trouble when I turned to the column headed "Private:" "M. X. begs the pretty Miss Z--, whom he met yesterday in Twenty-fifth Street omnibus, to come to him tomorrow, at his rooms, No. 17, St. Nicholas Hotel; he wishes to speak of marriage with her." What did the pretty Miss Z-- do? I don't even care to know.

I passed the whole of the afternoon in the grand saloon talking, and observing what was going on about me. Conversation could not fail to be interesting, for my friend Dean Pitferge was sitting near me.

"Have you quite recovered from the effects of your tumble?" I asked him.

“Perfectly," replied he, "but it's no go."

"What is no go? You?"

"No, our steam-ship; the screw boilers are not working well; we cannot get enough pressure."

"You are anxious, then, to get to New York?"

"Not in the least, I speak as an engineer, that is all. I am very comfortable here, and shall sincerely regret leaving this collection of originals which chance has thrown together for my recreation."

"Originals!" cried I, looking at the passengers who crowded the saloon; "but all those people are very much alike."

"Nonsense!” exclaimed the Doctor,"one can see you have hardly looked at them, the species is the same, I allow, but in that species what a variety there is I Just notice that group of men down there, with their easy-going air, their legs stretched on the sofas, and hats screwed down on their heads. They are Yankees, pure Yankees, from the small states of Maine, Vermont, and Connecticut, the produce of New England. Energetic and intelligent men, rather too much influenced by 'the Reverends,' and who have the disagreeable fault of never putting their hands before their mouths when they sneeze. Ah! my dear sir, they are true Saxons, always keenly alive to a bargain; put two Yankees in a room together, and in an hour they will each have gained ten dollars from the other."

" I will not ask how," replied I, smiling at the Doctor, "but among them I see a little man with a consequential air, looking like a weather-cock, and dressed in a long overcoat, with rather short black trousers,-who is that gentleman?"

“He is a Protestant minister, a man of 'importance' in Massachusetts, where he is going to join his wife, an exgoverness advantageously implicated in a celebrated lawsuit."

"And that tall, gloomy-looking fellow, who seems to be absorbed in calculation?"

"That man calculates: in fact," said the Doctor, "he is for ever calculating."

"Problems?"

"No, his fortune, he is a man of 'importance,' at any moment he knows almost to a farthing what he is worth; he is rich, a fourth part of New York is built on his land; a quarter of an hour ago he possessed 1,625,367 dollars and a half, but now he has only 1,625,367 dollars and a quarter."

"How came this difference in his fortune?"

"Well! He has just smoked a quarter-dollar cigar."

Doctor Dean Pitferge amused me with his clever repartees, so I pointed out to him another group stowed away in a corner of the saloon.

"They," said he, "are people from the Far West, the tallest, who looks like a head clerk, is a man of 'importance,' the head of a Chicago bank, he always carries an album under his arm, with the principal views of his beloved city. He is, and has reason to be, proud of a city founded in a desert in 1836, which at the present day has a population of more than 400,000 souls. Near him you see a Californian couple, the young wife is delicate and charming, her well-polished husband was once a plough-boy, who one fine day turned up some nuggets. That gentleman-"

" Is a man of 'importance," said I.

"Undoubtedly," replied the Doctor, "for his assets count by the million."

" And pray who may this tall individual be, who moves his head backwards and forwards like the pendulum of a clock?"

"That person," replied the Doctor, " is the celebrated Cockburn of Rochester, the universal statician, who has weighed, measured, proportioned, and calculated everything. Question this harmless maniac, he will tell you how much bread a man of fifty has eaten in his life, and how many cubic feet of air he has breathed. He will tell you how many volumes in quarto the words of a Temple lawyer would fill, and how many miles the postman goes daily carrying nothing but love-letters; he will tell you the number of widows who pass in one hour over London Bridge, and what would be the height of a pile of sandwiches consumed by the citizens of the Union in a year; he will tell you-"

The Doctor, in his excitement, would have continued for a long time in this strain, but other passengers passing us were attracted by the inexhaustible stock of his original remarks. What different characters there were in this crowd of passengers! Not one idler, however, for one does not go from one continent to the other without some serious motive. The most part of them were undoubtedly going to seek their fortunes on American ground, forgetting that at twenty years of age a Yankee has made his fortune, and that at twenty-five he is already too old to begin the struggle.

Among these adventurers, inventors, and fortune-hunters, Dean Pitferge pointed out to me some singularly interesting characters. Here was a chemist, a rival of Dr. Liebig, who pretended to have discovered the art of condensing all the nutritious parts of a cow into a meat-tablet, no larger than a five-shilling piece. He was going to coin money out of the cattle of the Pampas. Another, the inventor of a portable motive-power-a steam horse in a watch-case was going to exhibit his patent in New England. Another, a Frenchman from the "Rue Chapon," was carrying to America 30,000 cardboard dolls, which said "papa" with a very successful Yankee accent, and he had no doubt but that his fortune was made.

But besides these originals, there were still others whose secrets we could not guess; perhaps among them was some cashier flying from his empty cash-box, and a detective making friends with him, only waiting for the end of the passage to take him by the collar; perhaps also we might have found in this crowd clever genii who always find people ready to believe in them, even when they advocate the affairs of "The Oceanic Company for lighting Polynesia with gas," or " The Royal Society for making incombustible coal."

But at this moment my attention was attracted by the entrance of a young couple who seemed to be under the influence of a precocious weariness. "They are Peruvians, my dear sir," said the Doctor, "a couple married a year ago, who have been to all parts of the world for their honeymoon. They adored each other in Japan, loved in Australia, bore with one another in India, bored each other in France, quarreled in England, and will undoubtedly separate in America."

"And," said I, "who is that tall, haughty-looking man just coming in? From his appearance I should take him for an officer."

"He is a Mormon," replied the doctor, "an elder, Mr. Hatch, one of the great preachers in the city of Saints, What a fine type of manhood he is! Look at his proud eye, his noble countenance, and dignified bearing, so different from the Yankee. Mr. Hatch is returning from Germany and England, where he has preached Mormonism with great success, for there are numbers of this sect in Europe, who are allowed to conform to the laws of their country."

"Indeed!" said I; "I quite thought that polygamy was forbidden them in Europe."

"Undoubtedly, my dear sir, but do not think that polygamy is obligatory on Mormons; Brigham Young has his harem, because it suits him, but all his followers do not imitate him, not even those dwelling on the banks of the Salt Lake."

"Indeed! and Mr. Hatch?"

"Mr. Hatch has only one wife, and he finds that quite enough; besides, he proposes to explain his system in a meeting that he will hold one of these evenings."

"The saloon will be filled."

"Yes," said Pitferge, "if the gambling does not attract too many of the audience; you know that they play in a room at the bows? There is an Englishman there with an evil, disagreeable face, who seems to take the lead among them, he is a bad man, with a detestable reputation. Have you noticed him?"

From the Doctor's description, I had no doubt but that he was the same man who that morning had made himself conspicuous by his foolish wagers with regard to the waif. My opinion of him was not wrong. Dean Pitferge told me his name was Harry Drake, and that he was the son of a merchant at Calcutta, a gambler, a dissolute character, a duelist, and now that he was almost ruined, he was most likely going to America to try a life of adventures. "Such people," added the Doctor, "always find followers willing to flatter them, and this fellow has already formed his circle of scamps, of which he is the center. Among them I have noticed a little short man, with a round face, a turned-up nose, wearing gold spectacles, and having the appearance of a German

Jew; he calls himself a doctor, on the way to Quebec; but I take him for a low actor and one of Drake's admirers."

At this moment Dean Pitferge, who easily skipped from one subject to another, nudged my elbow. I turned my head towards the saloon door: a young man about twenty-eight, and a girl of seventeen, were coming in arm in arm. "A newly-married pair?" asked I.

"No," replied the Doctor, in a softened tone, "an engaged couple, who are only waiting for their arrival in New York to get married, they have just made the tour of Europe, of course with their family's consent, and they know now that they are made for one another. Nice young people; it is a pleasure to look at them. I often see them leaning over the railings of the engine-rooms, counting the turns of the wheels, which do not go half fast enough for their liking. Ah I sir, if our boilers were heated like those two youthful hearts, see how our speed would increase!"

CHAPTER XI

This day, at half-past twelve, a steersman posted up on the grand saloon door the following observation :

Lat. 51° I5' N.

Long. I 8° I 3' W.

Dist.: Fastenet, 323 miles.

This signified that at noon we were three hundred and twenty-three miles from the Fastenet lighthouse, the last which we had passed on the Irish coast, and at 51° 15' north latitude, and 18° 13' west longitude, from the meridian of Greenwich. It was the ship's bearing, which the captain thus made known to the passengers every day. By consulting this bearing, and referring it to a chart, the course of the *Great Eastern* might be followed. Up to this time she had only made three hundred and twenty miles in thirty six hours, it was not satisfactory, for a steamer at its ordinary speed does not go less than three hundred miles in twenty-four hours.

After having left the Doctor, I spent the rest of the day with Fabian; we had gone to the stern, which Pitfetge called "walking in the country." There alone, and leaning over the taffrail, we surveyed the great expanse of water, while around us rose the briny vapors distilled from the spray; small rainbows, formed by the refraction of the sun's rays, spanned the foaming waves. Below us, at a distance of forty feet, the screw was beating the water with a tremendous force, making its copper gleam in the midst of what appeared to be a vast conglomeration of liquefied emeralds, the fleecy track extending as far as the eye could reach, mingled in a milky path the foam from the screw, and the paddle engines, whilst the white and black fringed plumage of the sea-gulls flying above, cast rapid shadows over the sea.

Fabian was looking at the magic of the waves without speaking. What did he see in this liquid mirror, which gave scope to the most capricious flights of imagination? Was some vanished face passing before his eyes, and bidding him a last farewell? Did he see a drowning shadow in these eddying waters? He seemed to me sadder than usual, and I dared not ask him the cause of his grief.

After the long separation which had estranged us from each other, it was for him to confide in me, and for me to await his confidences. He had told me as much of his past life as he wished me to know; his life in the Indian garrison, his hunting, and adventures; but not a word had he said of the emotions which swelled in his heart, or the cause of the sighs which heaved his breast; undoubtedly Fabian was not one who tried to lessen his grief by speaking of it, and therefore he suffered the more.

Thus we remained leaning over the sea, and as I turned my head I saw the great paddles emerging under the regular action of the engine.

Once Fabian said to me, "This track is indeed magnificent. One would think that the waves were amusing themselves with tracing letters! Look at the 'l's' and 'e's'. Am I deceived? No, they are indeed always the same letter!"

Fabian's excited imagination saw in these eddyings that which it wished to see. But what could these letters signify? What remembrance did they call forth in Fabian's mind? The latter had resumed his silent contemplation, when suddenly he said to me,-

"Come to me, come; that gulf will draw me in!"

"What is the matter with you, Fabian," said I, taking him by both hands; " what is the matter, my friend?"

"I have here," said he, pressing his hand on his heart, "I have here a disease which will kill me."

"A disease?" said I to him, "a disease with no hope of cure?"

"No hope."

And without another word Fabian went to the saloon, and then on to his cabin.

CHAPTER XII

The next day, Saturday, 30th of March, the weather was fine, and the sea calm; our progress was more rapid, and the *Great Eastern* was now going at the rate of twelve knots an hour.

The wind had set south, and the first officer ordered the upper canvas to be hoisted, so that the ship was perfectly steady. Under this fine sunny sky the upper decks again became crowded: ladies appeared in fresh costumes, some walking about, others sitting down-I was going to say on the grass- plats beneath the shady trees, and the children resumed their interrupted games. With a few soldiers in uniform, strutting about with their hands in their pockets, one might have fancied oneself on a French promenade.

At noon, the weather being favorable, Captain Anderson and two officers went on to the bridge, in order to take the sun's altitude; each held a sextant in his hand, and from time to time scanned the southern horizon, towards which their horizon-glasses were inclined.

"Noon," exclaimed the Captain, after a short time. Immediately a steersman rang a bell on the bridge, and all the watches on board were regulated by the statement which had just been made.

Half-an-hour later, the following observation was posted up:-

Lat. 51° 10' N.

Long. 24° 13' W.

Course, 227 miles. Distance 550.

We had thus made two hundred and twenty-seven miles since noon the day before. I did not see Fabian once during the day. Several times, uneasy about his absence, I passed his cabin, and was convinced that he had not left it.

He must have wished to avoid the crowd on deck, and evidently sought to isolate himself from this tumult. I met Captain Corsican, and for an hour we walked on the poop. He often spoke of Fabian, and I could not help telling him what had passed between Fabian and myself the evening before.

"Yes," said Captain Corsican, with an emotion he did not try to disguise. "Two years ago Fabian had the right to think himself the happiest of men, and now he is the most unhappy." Archibald Corsican told me, in a few words, that at Bombay Fabian had known a charming young girl, a Miss Hodges. He loved her, and was beloved by her. Nothing seemed to hinder a marriage between Miss Hodges and Captain Mac Elwin; when, by her father's consent, the young girl's hand was sought by the son of a merchant at Calcutta. It was an old business affair, and Hodges, a harsh, obstinate, and unfeeling man, who happened at this time to be in a delicate position with his Calcutta correspondent, thinking that the marriage would settle everything well, sacrificed his daughter to the interests of his fortune. The poor child could not resist; they put her hand into that of the man she did not and could not love, and who, from all appearance; had no love for her. It was a mere business transaction, and a barbarous deed. The husband carried off his wife the day after they were married, and since then Fabian has never seen her whom he had always loved. This story showed me clearly that the grief which seemed to oppress Fabian was indeed serious.

"What was the young girl's name?" asked I of Captain Corsican.

"Ellen Hodges," replied he.

"Ellen,-that name explains the letters which Fabian thought he saw yesterday in the ship's track. And what is the name of this poor young woman's husband? said I to the Captain.

"Harry Drake."

"Drake!" cried I, "but that man is on board."

"He here!" exclaimed Corsican, seizing my hand, and looking straight at me.

"Yes," I replied, "he is on board."

"Heaven grant that they may not meet!" said the Captain gravely. "Happily they do not know each other, at least Fabian does not know Harry Drake; but that name uttered in his hearing would be enough to cause an outburst."

I then related to Captain Corsican what I knew of Harry Drake, that is to say, what Dr. Dean Pitferge had told me of him. I described him such as he was, an insolent, noisy adventurer, already ruined by gambling, and other vices, and ready to do anything to get money; at this moment Harry Drake passed close to us; I pointed him out to the Captain, whose eyes suddenly grew animated, and he made an angry gesture, which I arrested.

"Yes," said he, "there is the face of a villain. But where is he going?"

"To America, they say, to try and get by chance what he does not care to work for."

"Poor Ellen!" murmured the Captain; "where is she now?"

"Perhaps this wretch has abandoned her, or why should she not be on board?" said Corsican, looking at me.

This idea crossed my mind for the first time, but I rejected it. No; Ellen was not, could not be on board; she could not have escaped Dr. Pitferge's inquisitive eye. No; she cannot have accompanied Drake on this voyage!

"May what you say be true, sir! " replied Captain Corsican; "for the sight of that poor victim reduced to so much misery would be a terrible blow to Fabian: for I do not know what would happen, for Fabian is a man who would kill Drake like a dog. I ask you, as a proof of your friendship, never to lose sight of him; so that if anything should happen, one of us may be near, to throw ourselves between him and his enemy. You understand a duel must not take place between these two men. Alas I neither here nor elsewhere. A woman cannot marry her husband's murderer, however unworthy that husband may have been."

I well understood Captain Corsican's reason. Fabian could not be his own justiciary. It was foreseeing, from a distance, coming events, but how is it that the uncertainty of human things is so little taken into account? A presentiment was boding in my mind. Could it be possible, that in this common life on board, in this every-day mingling together, that Drake's noisy personality could remain unnoticed by Fabian? An accident, a trifle, a mere name uttered, would it not bring them face to face? Ah I how I longed to hasten the speed of the steamer which carried them both! Before leaving Captain Corsican I promised to keep a watch on our friend, and to observe Drake, whom on his part he engaged not to lose sight of; then he shook my hand, and we parted.

Towards evening a dense mist swept over the ocean, and the darkness was intense. The brilliantly-lighted saloons contrasted singularly with the blackness of the night. Waltzes and ballad songs followed each other; all received with frantic applause, and even hurrahs were not wanting, when the actor from T--, sitting at the piano, bawled his songs with the self- possession of a strolling player.

CHAPTER XIII

The next day, the 31st of March, was Sunday. How would this day be kept on board? Would it be the English or American Sunday, which closes the "bars" and the "taps" during service hours; which withholds the butcher's hand from his victim; which keeps the baker's shovel from the oven; which causes a suspension of business; extinguishes the fires of the manufactories; which closes the shops, opens the churches, and moderates the speed of the railway trains, contrary to the customs in France? Yes, it must be kept thus, or almost thus.

First of all, during the service, although the weather was fine, and we might have gained some knots, the Captain did not order the sails to be hoisted, as it would have been "improper." I thought myself very fortunate that the screw was allowed to continue its work, and when I inquired of a fierce Puritan the reason for this tolerance, "Sir," said he to me, "that which comes directly from God must be respected; the wind is in His hand, the steam is in the power of man."

I was willing to content myself with this reason, and in the meantime observed what was going on on board.

All the crew were in full uniform, and dressed with extreme propriety. I should not have been surprised to see the stokers working in black clothes; the officers and engineers wore their finest uniforms, with gilt buttons; their shoes shone with a British lustre, and rivaled their glazed hats with an intense irradiation. All these good people seemed to have hats and boots of a dazzling brightness. The Captain and the first officer set the example, and with new gloves and military attire, glittering and perfumed, they paced up and down the bridges awaiting the hour for service.

The sea was magnificent and resplendent beneath the first rays of a spring sun; not a sail in sight. The *Great Eastern* occupied alone the center of the immense expanse. At ten o'clock the bell on deck tolled slowly and at regular intervals; the ringer, who was a helmsman, dressed in his best, managed to obtain from this bell a kind of solemn, religious tone, instead of the metallic peals with which it accompanied the whistling of the boilers, when the ship was surrounded by fog. Involuntarily one looked for the village steeple which was calling to prayer. At this moment numerous groups appeared at the doors of the cabins, at the bows and stern; the boulevards were soon filled with men, women, and children carefully dressed for the occasion. Friends exchanged quiet greetings; every one held a Prayer-book in his hand, and all were waiting for the last bell which would announce the beginning of service. I saw also piles of Bibles, which were to be distributed in the church, heaped upon trays generally used for sandwiches.

The church was the great saloon, formed by the upper deck at the stern, the exterior of which, from its width and regularity of structure, reminded one very much of the hotel of the Ministere des Finances, in the Rue de Rivoli. I entered. Numbers of the faithful were already in their places. A profound silence reigned among the congregation; the officers occupied the apses of the church, and, in the midst of them, stood Captain Anderson, as pastor. My friend Dean Pitferge was near him, his quick little eyes running over the whole assembly. I will venture to say he was there more out of curiosity than anything else.

At half-past ten the Captain rose, and the service began; he read a chapter from the Old Testament. After each verse the congregation murmured the one following; the shrill soprano voices of the women and children distinctly separate from the baritone of the men. This Biblical dialogue lasted for about half-an-hour, and the simple, at the same time impressive ceremony, was performed with a puritanical gravity. Captain Anderson assuming the office of pastor on board, in the midst of the vast ocean, and speaking to a crowd of listeners, hanging, as it were, over the verge of an abyss, claimed the respect and attention of the most indifferent. It would have been well if the service had concluded with the reading; but when the Captain had finished a speaker arose, who could not fail to arouse feelings of violence and rebellion where tolerance and meditation should reign.

It was the reverend gentleman of whom I have before spoken-a little, fidgety man, an intriguing Yankee; one of those ministers who exercise such a powerful influence over the States of New England. His sermon was already prepared, the occasion was good, and he intended to make use of it. Would not the good Yorrick have done the same? I looked at Dean Pitferge; the Doctor did not frown, but seemed inclined to try the preacher's zeal.

The latter gravely buttoned his black overcoat, placed his silk cap on the table, drew out his handkerchief, with which he touched his lips lightly, and taking in the assembly at a glance-

" In the beginning," said he, "God created America, and rested on the seventh day." . . . .

Thereupon I reached the door.

CHAPTER XIV

At lunch Dean Pitferge told me that the reverend gentleman had admirably enlarged on his text. Battering rams, armed forts, and submarine torpedoes had figured in his discourse; as for himself, he was made great by the greatness of America. If it pleases America to be thus extolled, I have nothing to say.

Entering the grand saloon, I read the following note :

Lat. 50° 8' N.

Long. 30° 44' W,

Course, 255 miles.

Always the same result. We had only made eleven hundred miles, including the three hundred and ten between Fastenet and Liverpool, about a third part of our voyage. During the remainder of the day officers, sailors, and passengers continued to rest in accordance with established custom. Not a piano sounded in the silent saloons; the chess-men did not leave their box, or the cards their case; the billiard-room was deserted I had an opportunity this day to introduce Dean Pitferge to Captain Corsican. My original very much amused the Captain by telling him the stories whispered about the *Great Eastern.* He attempted to prove to him that it was a bewitched ship, to which fatal misfortune must happen. The yarn of the melted engineer greatly pleased the Captain, who, being a Scotsman, was a lover of the marvelous, but he could not repress an incredulous smile.

"I see," said Dr. Pitferge, "the Captain has not much faith in my stories."

"Much I that is saying a great deal," replied Corsican.

"Will you believe me, Captain, if I affirm that this ship is haunted at night?" asked the Doctor, in a serious tone.

"Haunted I" cried the Captain; "what next? Ghosts? And you believe in them?"

"I believe," replied Pitferge, " I believe what people who can be depended on have told me. Now, I know some of the officers on watch, and the sailors also, are quite unanimous on this point, that during the darkness of the night a shadow, a vague form, walks the ship. How it comes there they do not know, neither do they know how it disappears."

"By St. Dunstan! " exclaimed Captain Corsican, "we will watch it well together."

"Tonight?" asked the Doctor.

"Tonight, if you like; and you, sir," added the Captain, turning to me, "will you keep us company?"

"No," said I; " I do not wish to trouble the solitude of this phantom; besides, I would rather think that our Doctor is joking."

"I am not joking," replied the obstinate Pitferge.

"Come, Doctor," said I. "Do you really believe in the dead coming back to the decks of ships?"

"I believe in the dead who come to life again," replied the Doctor, and this is the more astonishing as I am a physician."

"A physician!" cried the Captain, drawing back as if the word had made him uneasy.

"Don't be alarmed, Captain," said the Doctor, smiling, good-humouredly; "I don't practice while traveling"

CHAPTER XV

The next day, the 1st of April, the aspect of the sea was truly spring-like; it was as green as the meadows beneath the sun's rays. This April sunrise on the Atlantic was superb; the waves spread themselves out voluptuously, while porpoises gambolled in the ship's milky track.

When I met Captain Corsican, he informed me that the ghost announced by the Doctor had not thought proper to make its appearance. Undoubtedly, the night was not dark enough for it. Then the idea crossed my mind that it was a joke of Dean Pitferge's, sanctioned by the 1st of April; for in America, England, and France this custom is very popular. Mystifiers and mystified were not wanting; some laughed, others were angry; I even believe that blows were exchanged among some of the Saxons, but these blows never ended in fighting; for it is well known that in England duels are liable to very severe punishment; even officers and soldiers are not allowed to fight under any pretext whatever. The homicide is subject to the most painful and ignominious punishments. I remember the Doctor telling me the name of an officer who was sent to a convict prison, for ten years, for having mortally wounded his adversary in a very honourable engagement. One can understand, that in face of this severe law duels have entirely disappeared from British customs.

The weather being so fine, a good observation could be made, which resulted in the following statement: Lat. 48° 47', and 36° 48' W. L.; dist., 250 miles only. The slowest of the Transatlantic steamers would have had the right to offer to take us in tow. This state of things very much annoyed Captain Anderson. The engineers attributed the failure of pressure to the insufficient ventilation of the new furnaces; but for my part, I thought that the diminution of speed was owing to the diameter of the wheels having been imprudently made smaller.

However, today, about two o'clock, there was an improvement in the ship's speed; it was the attitude of the two young lovers which revealed this change to me. Leaning against the bulwarks, they murmured joyful words, clapped their hands, and looked smilingly at the escape-pipes, which were placed near the funnels, the apertures of which were crowned with a white wreath of vapor The pressure had risen in the screw boilers; as yet it was only a feeble breath of air, a wavering blast;

but our young friends drank it in eagerly with their eyes. No, not even Denis Papin could have been more delighted, when he saw the steam half raise the lid of his celebrated saucepan.

"They smoke! They smoke!" cried the young lady, whilst a light breath also escaped from her parted lips.

" Let us go and look at the engine," said the young man, placing her arm in his.

Dean Pitferge had joined me, and we followed the loving couple on to the upper-deck.

"How beautiful is youth!" remarked the Doctor.

"Yes," said I, "youth affianced."

Soon we also were leaning over the railing of the engine rooms. There, in the deep abyss, at a distance of sixty feet below us, we saw the four long horizontal pistons swaying one towards the other, and with each movement moistened by drops of lubricating oil.

In the meanwhile the young man had taken out his watch, and the girl, leaning over his shoulder, followed the movement of the minute-hand, whilst her lover counted the revolutions of the screw.

"One minute," said she.

"Thirty-seven turns," exclaimed the young man.

"Thirty-seven and a half," observed the Doctor, who had entered into the work.

"And a half," cried the young lady. "You hear, Edward I Thank you, sir," said she, favouring the worthy Pitferge with one of her most pleasing smiles.

CHAPTER XVI

Going back to the grand saloon, I saw the following programme posted on the door:

THIS NIGHT!

PART FIRST

" Ocean Time" . . . *Mr. Mac Alpine,*

Song: "Beautiful Isle of the Sea" . . . *Mr. Ewing.*

Reading . . . *Mr. Afflect.*

Piano solo: "Chant du Berger" . . . *Mrs. Alloway*

Scot.ch Song . . . *Doctor T--.*

(*Ten minutes interval.)*

PART SECOND

Piano solo . . . *Mr. Paul V--.*

Burlesque: "Lady of Lyons" . . . *Doctor T--.*

Entertainment . . . *Sir James Anderson.*

Song: "Happy Moment" . . . *Mr. Norville.*

Song: " You Remember" . . . *Mr. Ewing.*

FINALE.

"GOD SAVE THE QUEEN."

As may be seen, it was a complete concert, with a first part, entr'acte, second part, and finale; but it seems there was something wanting in the programme; for I heard some one mutter behind me, "What! No Mendelssohn."

I turned, and saw that it was a steward, who thus protested against the omission of his favourite music.

I went on deck, and began to look for Mac Elwin. Corsican had just told me that Fabian had left his cabin, and I wanted, without intruding myself on him, to draw him out of his isolation. I found him at the bows; we talked for some time, but he made no allusion to his past life. At times he was silent and pensive, absorbed in his thoughts, no longer listening to me, and pressing his breast, as if to restrain a painful spasm.

Whilst we were walking together, Harry Drake passed us several times, always the same noisy, gesticulating man, obstructive as would be a windmill in a ball-room. Was I mistaken? I could not say; for I had already anticipated it in my mind; but it seemed to me that Harry Drake stared at Fabian with a persistency which the latter must have noticed; for he said to me,-

"Who is that man?"

"I don't know," I replied.

"I don't like his looks," added Fabian.

Put two ships in the open sea, without wind or tide, and, at last, they will come together. Throw two planets into space, and they will fall one on the other. Place two enemies in the midst of a crowd, and they will inevitably meet; it is a fatality, a question of time, that is all.

In the evening the concert took place according to the programme; the grand saloon, filled with the audience, was brilliantly lighted. Through the half-open hatchways might be seen the broad, sunburnt faces, and the great black hands of the sailors; the doorways were crowded with stewards; the greater part of the audience-men and women-were seated on side sofas, and in the center of the saloon, in arm-chairs and lounges, all facing the piano, firmly fastened between the two doors, which opened into the ladies' saloon. From time to time a rolling motion disturbed the. audience; arm-chairs and folding-chairs glided about, a kind of swell caused a similar undulatory movement to all; they caught hold of one another silently, and without making any joke; but upon the whole there was not much fear of falling, thanks to the subsidence.

The concert opened with the *Ocean Times*. The *Ocean Times* was a daily newspaper, political, commercial, and literary, which certain passengers had started for the requirements on board. Americans and English took to this sort of pastime; they wrote out their sheet during the day; and let me say, that if the editors were not particular, as to the quality of their articles, their readers were not more so. They were content with little, even with "not enough."

This number for the 1st of April contained a *Great Eastern* leader-tame enough, on general politics-also various facts quite uninteresting to a Frenchman; articles on the money-markets, not particularly comic;

curious telegrams, and some rather insipid home news. After all this kind of fun is only amusing to those who make it. The Honourable Mac Alpine, a dogmatical American, read, with earnest gravity, some rather dull lucubrations, which were received by his audience with great applause. He finished his reading with the following news; "It is announced that President Johnson has resigned in favour of General Grant."

"It is said that Fernando Cortez is going to attack the Emperor Napoleon the Third, piratically, out of revenge for the latter's conquest of Mexico."

"We are told for a certainty that Pope Pius IX has designated the Prince Imperial as his successor."

When the *Ocean Times* had been sufficiently applauded, the Honourable Mr. Ewing, a fine-looking young fellow, with a tenor voice, warbled "Beautiful Isle of the Sea," with all the harshness of an English throat.

The "reading" appeared to me to have a questionable charm; it was simply two or three pages of a book, read by a worthy Texan, who began in a low voice, and gradually got higher and higher; he also was very much applauded.

The "Shepherd's Song," a piano solo, by Mrs. Alloway, and a Scotch song, sung by Doctor T--, concluded the first part of the programme.

After the ten minutes' interval, during which some of the audience left their seats, the second part of the concert began. The Frenchman, Paul V --, played some charming waltzes, which were noisily encored. One of the ship's doctors on board, a very conceited young man, recited a burlesque scene, a kind of parody on the "Lady of Lyons," a drama very much in vogue in England.

The "burlesque" was succeeded by the "entertainment." What had Sir James Anderson prepared under this name? Was it a conference or a sermon? Neither the one nor the other. Sir James Anderson rose smilingly, drew a pack of cards from his pocket, turned back his white cuffs, and performed some tricks, the simplicity of which was redeemed by the graceful manner in which they were done. - Hurrahs and applause.

After the *Happy Moment*, and *You Remember*,' sung by Mr. Norville and Mr. Ewing, the programme announced *God Save the Queen*; but some Americans begged Paul V-, as he was a Frenchman, to play the national French Anthem. Immediately my agreeable countryman began the inevitable *Partant pour la Syrie*. Energetic demands from a party of north-men, who wished to hear the *Marseillaise*, and without being pressed further, the obedient pianist, with a compliance which betokened rather a musical facility than political convictions, vigorously attacked the song of Rouget de l'Ile.

This was the grand success of the evening, and the assembly, standing, slowly sang the "National Anthem,"which prays God to bless the Queen.

Upon the whole this soiree was as good as amateur soirees generally are; that is to say, it was chiefly a success for the performers and their friends. Fabian did not show himself there at all.

CHAPTER XVII

During Monday night the sea was very stormy. Once more the partitions began creaking, and again the luggage made its way through the saloons. When I went on deck, about seven o'clock in the morning, the wind had freshened, and it was raining. The officer on watch had ordered the sails to be taken in, so that the steam-ship, left without any support, rolled dreadfully. All this day, the 2nd of April, the deck was deserted, even the saloons were empty, for the passengers had taken refuge in their cabins; and two-thirds of the guests were missing at lunch and dinner. Whist was impossible, for the tables glided from under the players' hands. The chess- en were unmanageable. A few of the more fearless stretched themselves on the sofas, reading or sleeping, as many preferred to brave the rain on deck, where the sailors, in their oil-skin jackets and glazed hats, were sedately pacing to and fro. The first officer, well wrapped in his macintosh, and perched on the bridge, was on watch, and in the midst of the hurricane his small eyes sparkled with delight This was what the little man loved, and the steamer rolled to his liking. The water from the skies and sea mingled in a dense fog. The atmosphere was grey, and birds flew screeching through the damp mists. At ten o'clock a three-mast ship was hailed, sailing astern of us, but her nationality could not be recognized. At about eleven o'clock the wind abated, and veered to the north-west. The rain ceased, almost suddenly, blue sky appeared through the opening in the clouds, the sun shone out again, and permitted a more or less perfect observation to be made, which was posted up as follows :-

Lat. 46' 29' N.

Long. 42° 25' W.

Dist., 356 miles.

So that, although the pressure of the boilers had risen, the ship's speed had not increased; but this might be attributed to the westerly wind, which caught the ship ahead, and considerably impeded her progress.

At two o'clock the fog grew dense again, the wind fell and rose at the same time. The thickness of the fog was so intense that the officers on the bridge could not see the men at the bows. These accumulated vapors rising from the sea constitute the greatest danger of navigation.

They cause accidents which it is impossible to avoid, and a collision at sea is more to be dreaded than a fire.

Thus, in the midst of the fog, officers and sailors were obliged to keep a strict watch, which soon proved to be necessary, for about three o'clock a three-master appeared at less than two hundred yards from the *Great Eastern,* her sails disabled by a gust of wind, and no longer answering to her helm. The *Great Eastern* turned in time to avoid her, thanks to the promptitude with which the men on watch warned the steersman. These well-regulated signals are given by means of a bell, fastened to the poop at the bows. One ring signifies ship a-head; two, ship on starboard bow; three, ship on port bow; and immediately the man at the helm steers in order to avoid a collision.

The wind did not abate until evening; however the rolling was nothing to speak of, as the sea was protected by the Newfoundland heights. Another entertainment, by Sir James Anderson, was announced for this day. At the appointed hour the saloon was filled; but this time it had nothing to do with cards. Sir James Anderson told us the history of the Transatlantic Cable, which he had himself laid. He showed us photographs representing the different engines used for the immersion. He sent round a model of the splice which was used to fasten together the pieces of cable. Finally, very justly merited, the three cheers with which his lecture received, a great part of which was meant for the Honourable Cyrus Field, promoter of the enterprise, who was present on this occasion.

CHAPTER XVIII

The next day, the 3rd of April, from early dawn the horizon wore that peculiar aspect which the English call "blink." It was of that misty white colour which signifies that icebergs are not far distant; in fact the *Great Eastern* was ploughing those seas on which float the first blocks of ice detached from the icebergs in Davis' Straits. A special watch was kept, in order to avoid the rude collision with these enormous blocks.

There was a strong westerly wind blowing; strips of clouds, or rather shreds of vapor, hung over the sea, through which glimpses of blue sky appeared. A dull thudding noise came from the waves tossed by the wind, and drops of water, seemingly pulverized, evaporated in foam.

Neither Fabian, Captain Corsican, nor Doctor Pitferge had yet come on deck, so I went towards the bows, where the junction of the bulwarks formed a comfortable angle, a kind of retreat, in which like a hermit, one could retire from the world. I took my place in this corner, sitting on a skylight, and my feet resting on an enormous pulley; the wind being dead ahead passed over without touching me. This was a good place for reflection. From here I had a view of the whole immensity of the ship; I could see the long slanting ropes of the rigging at the stern. On the first level a top-man, hanging in the mizenshrouds, held himself up with one hand, whilst with the other he worked with a remarkable dexterity. On the deck below him paced the officer on watch, peering through the mists. On the bridge, at the stern, I caught a glimpse of an officer, his back rounded, and his head muffled in a hood, struggling against the gusts of wind. I could distinguish nothing of the sea, except a bluish horizontal line discernible behind the paddles. Urged on by her powerful engines, the narrow stem of the steam-ship cut the waves, with a hissing sound, like that when the sides of a boiler are heated by a roaring fire. But the colossal ship, with the wind a-head, and borne on three waves, hardly felt the movement of the sea, which would have shaken any other steamer with its pitchings.

At half-past twelve the notice stated that we were in 44° 53' North lat., and 47° 6' W. long., and had made two hundred and twenty-seven miles in twenty-four hours only. The young couple must have scolded the wheels which did not turn, and the steam which was not at all strong enough to please them.

About three o'clock the sky, swept by the wind, cleared up; the line of the horizon was once more clearly defined, the wind fell, but for a long while the sea rose in great foam crested billows. Such a gentle breeze could not cause this swell; one might have said that the Atlantic was still sulky.

At twenty-five minutes to four . a three-mast ship was hailed to larboard. She hoisted her name; it was the *Illinois*, an American ship, on her way to England.

At this moment Lieutenant H-- informed me that we were passing Cape Race point. We were now in the rich coasts where are obtained cod-fish, three of which would suffice to supply England and America if all the roe were hatched. The day passed without any remarkable occurrence; no accident had as yet thrown Fabian and Harry Drake together, for the Captain and I never lost sight of them. In the evening the same harmless amusement, the same reading, and songs in the grand saloon called forth, as usual, frantic applauses. As an extraordinary occurrence a lively discussion broke out between a Northerner and a Texan. The latter demanded an Emperor for the Southern States. Happily this political discussion, which threatened to degenerate into a quarrel, was put an end to by the timely arrival of an imaginary dispatch, addressed to the *Ocean Times*, and conceived in these terms: "Captain Semmes, Minister of War, has made the South compensate for its ravages in Alabama."

CHAPTER XIX

Leaving the brilliantly lighted saloon I went on deck with Captain Corsican. The night was dark; not a star in the firmament; an impenetrable gloom surrounded the ship. The windows of the saloon shone like the mouths of furnaces; the man on watch, heavily pacing the poop, was scarcely discernible, but one could breathe the fresh air, and the Captain inhaled it with expanded lungs.

"I was stifled in the saloon," said he; "here at least I can breathe. I require my hundred cubic yards of pure air every twenty-four hours, or I get half suffocated."

"Breathe, Captain, breathe at your ease," said I to him ; "the breeze does not stint your wants. Oxygen is a good thing, but it must be confessed Parisians and Londoners know it only by reputation."

" Yes," replied the Captain, " and they prefer carbonic acid. Ah well I every one to his liking; for my own part I detest it, even in champagne."

Thus talking, we paced up and down the deck on the starboard side, sheltered from the wind by the high partitions of the deck cabins. Great wreaths of smoke, illuminated with sparks, curled from the black chimneys; the noise of the engines accompanied the whistling of the wind in the shrouds, which sounded like the cords of a harp. Mingling with this hubbub, each quarter of an hour, came the cry of the sailors on deck, "All's well, all's well."

In fact no precaution had been neglected to insure the safety of the ship on these coasts frequented by icebergs. The Captain had a bucket of water drawn every half hour, in order to ascertain the temperature, and if it had fallen one degree he immediately changed his course, for he knew that the *Peruvian* had been seen but a fortnight since blocked up by icebergs in this latitude; it was therefore a danger to be avoided. His orders for night were to keep a strict look-out. He himself remained on the bridge with an officer each side of him, one at the paddle-wheel signal, the other at the screw signal; besides these a lieutenant and two men kept watch on the poop, whilst a quarter-master with a sailor stood at the stern; the passengers might therefore rest quietly.

After noticing these arrangements we went back again to the stern, as we had made up our minds to stay some time longer, walking on deck like peaceful citizens taking an evening stroll in their town squares.

The place seemed deserted. Soon, however, our eyes grew accustomed to the darkness, and we perceived a man leaning perfectly motionless, with his elbow on the railing. Corsican, after looking at him attentively for some time, said to me,-

"It is Fabian."

It was indeed Fabian. We recognized him, but absorbed as he was in a profound contemplation he did not see us. His eyes were fixed on an angle of the upper deck; I saw them gleam in the dark. What was he looking at? How could he pierce this black gloom? I thought it better to leave him to his reflections, but Captain Corsican went up to him.

"Fabian," said he.

Fabian did not answer; he had not heard. Again Corsican called him. He shuddered, and turned his head for a moment, saying,-

"Hush."

Then with his hand he pointed to a shadow which was slowly moving at the further end of the upper deck. It was this almost invisible figure that Fabian was looking at, and smiling sadly he murmured,-

"The black lady."

I shuddered. Captain Corsican took hold of my arm, and I felt that he also was trembling. The same thought had struck us both. This shadow was the apparition about which Dean Pitferge had spoken. Fabian had relapsed into his dreamy contemplation. I, with a heaving breast and awe-struck glance, looked at this human figure, the outline of which was hardly discernible; but presently it became more defined. It came forward, stopped, turned back, and then again advanced, seeming to glide rather than walk. At ten steps from us it stood perfectly still. I was then able to distinguish the figure of a slender female, closely wrapped in a kind of brown burnous, and her face covered with a thick veil.

"A mad woman, a mad woman, is it not?" murmured Fabian.

It was, indeed, a mad woman; but Fabian was not asking us: he was speaking to himself. In the meantime the poor creature came still nearer to us. I thought I could see her eyes sparkle through her veil, when they were fixed on Fabian. She went up to him, Fabian started to his feet, electrified. The veiled woman put her hand on her heart as though counting its pulsation, then, gliding swiftly away, she disappeared behind the angle of the upper deck. Fabian staggered, and fell on his knees, his hands stretched out before him.

"It is she," he murmured.

Then shaking his head,-

"What an hallucination!" he added.

Captain Corsican then took him by the hand.

"Come, Fabian, come," said he, and he led away his unhappy friend.

CHAPTER XX

Corsican and I could no longer doubt but that it was Ellen, Fabian's betrothed, and Harry Drake's wife. Chance had brought all three together on the same ship. Fabian had not recognized her, although he had cried, "It is she, it is she!" and how was it possible that he could have done so? But he was not mistaken in saying, "A mad woman!" Ellen was mad, undoubtedly; grief, despair, love frozen in her heart, contact with the worthless man who had snatched her from Fabian, ruin, misery, and shame bad broken her spirit. It was on this subject that Corsican and I spoke the following morning. We had no doubt as to the identity of the young woman; it was Ellen, whom Harry Drake was dragging with him to the American continent. The Captain's eyes glowed with a dark fire at the thought of this wretch, and I felt my heart stir within me. What were we against the husband, the master? Nothing. But now, what was most important, was to prevent another meeting between Fabian and Ellen, for Fabian could not fail at last to recognize his betrothed, and thus the catastrophe we wished to avoid would be brought about.

At the same time we had reason to hope that these two poor creatures would not see each other again, as the unhappy Ellen never appeared in the daytime, either in the saloons or on the deck. Only at night, perhaps eluding her gaoler, she came out to bathe herself in the damp air, and demand of the wind a smooth passage. In four days, at the latest, the *Great Eastern* must reach New York harbour; therefore we might hope that accident would not dally with our watchfulness, and that Fabian would not discover Ellen during this time ; but we made our calculations without thinking of events.

The steamer's course had been slightly altered in the night, three times the ship, being in water twenty-seven degrees Fahrenheit-that is to say, five degrees below zero, had been turned towards the south. There was no longer any doubt of icebergs being very near, for the sky that morning had a peculiarly brilliant aspect; the atmosphere was misty, and the northern sky glittered with an intense reverberation, evidently produced by the powerful reflection from the icebergs. There was a piercing wind, and about ten o'clock the deck was powdered by a slight snow-fall; then dense fog surrounded us, in which we gave warning of our approach, by deafening whistles, which scared away the flocks of sea-gulls in the ship's yards. At half-past ten, the fog having cleared off, a screw steamer appeared on the horizon, a-starboard, the white tops o(her chimneys indicating that she was an emigrant ship, belonging to the Inman Company.

Before lunch several of the passengers organized a pool, which could not fail to please those fond of betting and gambling. The result of this pool was not to be known for four days; it was what is called the "pilot's pool." When a ship arrives at the land-falls every one knows that a pilot comes on board; so they divide the twenty-four hours of the day and night into forty-eight half-hours, or ninety-six quarters, according to the number of the passengers. Each player stakes one dollar, and draws one of the half or quarter hours: the winner of the forty-eight or ninety-six dollars is the one during whose quarter of an hour the pilot comes on board. From this it may be seen that the game is very simple; it is not a race-course, but a quarter-of-an hour race.

It was a Canadian, the Honourable MacAlpine, who undertook the management of the affair. He easily collected ninety-six players, including several professed gamblers, not the least among those ready for gain. I, following the general example, staked my dollar, and fate allotted me the ninety-fourth quarter; it was a bad number, and one which left me no chance of profit. The fact is, these divisions are reckoned from noon to noon, so that there are night as well as day quarters; and as it is very seldom that ships venture close in in the dark, the chance of a pilot coming on board then is very small. However, I easily consoled myself. Going down into the saloon, I saw a lecture announced. The Utah missionary was going to hold a meeting on Mormonism; a good opportunity for those wishing to initiate themselves in the mysteries of the City of Saints; besides, this Elder, Mr. Hatch, was an orator of no mean power. The execution could not fail to be worthy of the work. The announcement of the conference was received very favourably by the passengers.

The observation posted up was as follows :-

Lat. 42° 32' N.

Long. 51° 59' W.

Course, 254 miles.

About three o'clock in the afternoon the steersman signaled a large four- mast steamer, which slightly changed its course, in order to give the Great Eastern its number. It was the *Atlanta*, one of the largest boats running between London and New York, calling at Brest on the way. After having saluted us, which we returned, in a short time she was out of sight.

At this moment Dean Pitferge, in a vexed tone, informed me that Mr. Hatch's lecture was forbidden, as the wives of the puritans on board did not approve of their husbands becoming acquainted with the mysteries of Mormonism.

CHAPTER XXI

At four o'clock, the sky, which had been overcast, cleared up, the sea grew calm, and the ship was so steady, one might almost have thought oneself on *terra firma*-this gave the passengers the idea of getting up races. Epsom turf could not have afforded a better coursing-ground, and as for horses, they were well replaced by pure Scotsmen, as good as any *Gladiator*, or *La Touque*. The news soon spread, sportsmen immediately hurried to the field. An Englishman, the Hon. J. Mac Carthy, was appointed commissioner, and the competitors presented themselves without delay. They were half a dozen sailors, kind of centaurs, man and horse at the same time, all ready to try for the prize.

The two boulevards formed the race-course, the runners were to go three times round the ship, thus making a course of about 1300 yards, which was quite enough. Soon the galleries were invaded by crowds of spectators, all armed with opera glasses. Some of them had hoisted the "green sail," no doubt to shelter themselves from the spray of the Atlantic. Carriages were missing. I must confess, but not the rank, where they might have ranged in file. Ladies in gay costumes were hurrying on to the upper-decks; the scene was charming.

Fabian, Captain Corsican, Dr. Pitferge and I had taken our places on the poop, which was what might be called the center of action. Here the real gentlemen riders were assembled; in front of us was the starting and winning post. Betting soon began with a true British animation. Considerable sums of money were staked, but only from the appearance of the racers, whose qualifications had not as yet been inscribed in the "stud-nook." It was not without uneasiness that I saw Harry Drake interfering in the preparations with his usual audacity, discussing, disputing, and settling affairs in a tone which admitted of no reply. Happily, although Fabian had risked some pounds in the race, he appeared quite indifferent to the noise; he kept himself aloof from the others, and it was quite evident his thoughts were far off.

Among the racers who offered themselves, two particularly attracted the public attention. Wilmore, a small, thin, wiry Scotsman, with a broad chest and sharp eyes, was one of the favourites; the other, an Irishman named O'Kelly, a tall, supple fellow, balanced the chance with Wilmore, in the eyes of connoisseurs. Three to one was asked on him, and for myself partaking the general infatuation, I was going to risk a few dollars on him, when the Doctor said to me,-

"Choose the little one; believe me, the tall one is no go."

" What do you say?"

"I say," replied the Doctor, "that the tall one is not genuine; he may have a certain amount of speed, but he has no bottom. The little one, on the contrary, is of pure Scottish race; look how straight his body is on his legs, and how broad and pliant his chest is; he is a man who will lead more than once in the race. Bet on him, I tell you; you won't regret it."

I took the learned doctor's advice, and bet on Wilmore; as to the other four, they were not even discussed.

They drew for places; chance favoured the Irishman, who had the rope-side; the six runners were placed along the line, bounded by the posts, so that there was no unfair start to be feared.

The commissioner gave the signal, and the departure was hailed by a loud hurrah. It was soon evident that Wilmore and O'Kelly were professional runners; without taking any notice of their rivals, who passed them breathless, they ran with their bodies thrown slightly forward, heads very erect, arms tightly pressed against their chests, and holding their fists firmly in front.

In the second round O'Kelly and Wilmore were in a line, having distanced their exhausted competitors. They obviously verified the Doctor's saying,-

"It is not with the legs, but with the chest that one runs; ham-strings are good, but lungs are better."

At the last turning but one the spectators again cheered their favourites. Cries and hurrahs broke out on all sides.

"The little one will win," said Pitferge to me." Look, he is not even panting, and his rival is breathless."

Wilmore indeed looked calm and pale, whilst O'Kelly was steaming like a damp hay-stack; he was "pumped out," to use a sportsman's slang expression, but both of them kept the same line. At last they passed the upper decks; the hatchway of the engine-rooms, the winning-post.

"Hurrah! Hurrah! For Wilmore," cried some.

"Hurrah! For O'Kelly," chimed in others.

"Wilmore has won."

"No, they are together."

The truth was Wilmore had won, but by hardly half a head so the Honourable Mac Carthy decided. However, the discussion continued, and even came to words. The partisans of the Irishman, and particularly Harry Drake, maintained that it was a " dead heat," and that they ought to go again.

But at this moment, urged by an irresistible impulse, Fabian went up to Harry Drake, and said to him in a cold tone,-

" You are wrong, sir, the winner was the Scott sailor."

"What do you say?" he asked, in a threatening tone.

"I say you are wrong," answered Fabian quietly.

"Undoubtedly," retorted Drake, "because you bet on Wilmore."

' I was for O'Kelly, like yourself; I lost, and I have paid."

"Sir," cried Drake, "do you pretend to teach me ?-"

But he did not finish his sentence, for Captain Corsican had interposed between him and Fabian, with the intention of taking up the quarrel. He treated Drake with supreme contempt, but evidently Drake would not pick a quarrel with him; so when Corsican had finished, he crossed his arms, and addressing himself to Fabian,-

" This gentleman," said he, with an evil smile, " this gentleman wants some one to fight his battles for him. Fabian grew pale, he would have sprung at Drake, but I held him back, and the scoundrel's companions dragged him away; not, however, before he had cast a look of hatred at his enemy.

Captain Corsican and I went below with Fabian, who contented himself by saying, "The first opportunity I have, I will box that impudent fellow's ears."

CHAPTER XXII

From Thursday night to Saturday the *Great Eastern* was crossing the Gulf Stream, the water of which is of a dark colour, the surface of the current forcing its way against the waters of the Atlantic, is even slightly convex. It is, in fact, a river running between two liquid shores, and one of the largest in the world, for it reduces the Amazon and Mississippi to mere brooks in comparison.

This day, the 5th of April, began with a magnificent sunrise, the waves glittered, and a warm south-west wind was wafted through the rigging. It was the beginning of the fine weather; the sun, which had clothed the fields of the continent with verdure, caused fresh costumes to bloom on board. Vegetation is sometimes behind-hand, but fashion never. Soon the Boulevards, filled with groups of promenaders, looked like the Champs Elysees on a fine Sunday afternoon in May.

I did not see Captain Corsican once that morning; wishing to hear of Fabian, I went to his cabin, and knocked at the door, but getting no answer I opened it and went in. Fabian was not there. I went on deck again, but could find neither my friends nor the Doctor; the idea then crossed my mind to find out where the unfortunate Ellen was confined. What cabin did she occupy? Where had Drake shut her up? In whose care was the poor creature left, when Drake abandoned her for whole days? Most likely with some disinterested stewardess, or an indifferent nurse. I wished to know how it was, not from any vain motive of curiosity, but simply in Ellen and Fabian's interest, if it was only to prevent a meeting, always to be dreaded.

I began my search with the cabin near the ladies' saloon, and went along the passages of both stories. This inspection was easy enough, as the names of the occupants were written on each door, in order to facilitate the steward's work. I did not see Harry Drake's name, but this did not surprise me. much, as I had no doubt he had preferred the more isolated cabins at the stern. In matter of comfort, however, no difference existed between the cabins at the bows and those at the stern, for the *Freighters* had only admitted one class of passengers.

I next went towards the dining saloons, keeping carefully to the side passages which wound between the double row of cabins. All these rooms were occupied, and all had the name of the passengers outside, but Harry Drake's name was not to be seen. This time the absence of his name astonished me, for I thought I had been all over our Floating City, and I was not aware of any part more secluded than this.

I inquired of a steward, who told me there were yet a hundred cabins behind the dining saloons.

"How do you get to them?" I asked.

"By a staircase at the end of the upper deck."

"Thank you, and can you tell me which cabin Mr. Harry Drake occupies ?"

"I do not know, sir," replied the steward.

Again I went on deck, and following the steward's direction at last came to the door at the top of the stairs. This staircase did not lead to any large saloons, but simply to a dimly-lighted landing, round which was arranged a double row of cabins. Harry Drake could hardly have found a more favorable place in which to hide Ellen.

The greater part of the cabins were unoccupied. I went along the landing, a few names were written on the doors, but only two or three at the most. Harry Drake's name was not among them, and as I had made a very minute inspection of this compartment, I was very much disappointed at my ill success. I was going away when suddenly a vague, almost inaudible murmur caught my ear, it proceeded from the left side of the passage. I went towards the place; the sounds, at first faint, grew louder, and I distinguished a kind of plaintive song, or rather melopceia, the words of which did not reach me.

I listened; it was a woman singing, but in this unconscious voice one could recognize a mournful wail. Might not this voice belong to the mad woman? My presentiments could not deceive me. I went quietly nearer to the cabin, which was numbered 775 It was the last in this dim passage, and must have been lighted by the lowest light-ports in the hull of the *Great Eastern*; there was no name on the door, and Harry Drake had no desire that any one should know the place where he confined Ellen.

I could not distinctly hear the voice of the unfortunate woman; her song was only a string of unconnected sentences like one speaking in sleep, but at the same time it was sweet and plaintive.

Although I had no means of recognizing her identity, I had no doubt but that it was Ellen singing. I listened for some minutes, and was just going away, when I heard a step on the landing. Could it be Harry Drake? I did not wish him to find me here, for Fabian and Ellen's sake; fortunately I could get on deck, without being seen, by a passage leading round the cabins. However, I stopped to know who it really was that I had heard. The darkness partially hid me, and standing behind an angle of the passage I could see without being myself in sight.

In the meantime the sound of the footsteps had ceased, and with it, as a strange coincident, Ellen's voice. I waited and soon the song began again, and the boards creaked under a stealthy tread; I leaned forward and, in the dim, uncertain light which glimmered through the creaks of the cabin doors, I recognized Fabian.

It was my unhappy friend! What instinct could have led him to this place? Had he then discovered the young woman's retreat before me? I did not know what to think. Fabian slowly advanced along the passage, listening, following the voice, as if it was a thread drawing him unconsciously on, and in spite of himself. It seemed to me that the song grew fainter as he approached, and that the thread thus held was about to break. Fabian went quite near to the cabin doors and then stopped.

How those sad accents must have rent his heart! And how his whole being must have thrilled as he caught some tone in the voice, which reminded him of the past! But how was it, ignorant as he was of Harry Drake being on board, that he had any suspicion of Ellen's presence? No, it was impossible; he had only been attracted by the plaintive accents which insensibly responded to the great grief weighing down his spirit.

Fabian was still listening. What was he going to do?

Would he call to the mad woman? And what if Ellen suddenly appeared? Everything was dangerous in this situation! However, Fabian came nearer still to the door of her cabin; the song, which was growing fainter and fainter, suddenly died away, and a piercing shriek was heard.

Had Ellen, by a magnetic communication, felt him whom she loved so near her? Fabian's attitude was desperate; he had gathered himself up. Was he going to break the door open? I thought he would, so I rushed up to him.

He recognized me; I dragged him away, and he made no resistance, but asked me in a hollow voice, " Do you know who that unhappy woman is?"

"No, Fabian, no."

"It is the mad woman," said he, in an unnatural tone, "but this madness is not without remedy. I feel that a little devotion, a little love, would cure the poor woman."

"Come, Fabian," said I, "come away."

We went on deck, but Fabian did not utter another word. I did not leave him, however, until he had reached his cabin.

CHAPTER XXIII

Some moments later I met Captain Corsican, and told him of the scene I had just witnessed. He understood, as well as I did, that the situation of affairs was growing more and more serious. Ah I could I have foreseen all that would happen, how I should have longed to hasten the speed of the *Great Eastern,* and put the broad ocean between Fabian and Harry Drake!

On leaving each other, Captain Corsican and I agreed to watch the actors in this drama more narrowly than ever.

The *Australasian*, a Cunard steamer, running between Liverpool and New York, was expected this day. She was to leave America on Wednesday morning, and therefore would not be long before passing us. A watch was kept; however, she did not come in sight.

About eleven o'clock the English passengers organized a subscription on behalf of the wounded on board, some of whom had not been able to leave the hospital; among them was the boatswain, threatened with an incurable lameness. There was soon a long list of signatures, not however, without some objections having been raised.

At noon a very exact observation was able to be made-Long.

58°, 37' W.

Lat 41° 41' II" N.

Course, 257 miles.

We had the latitude to a second. When the young engaged couple read the notice they did not look remarkably pleased, and they had good reason to be discontented with the steam.

Before lunch, Captain Anderson wishing to divert the passengers from the tedium of their long voyage, arranged some gymnastic exercises, which he directed in person. About fifty unemployed men, each armed like himself, with a stick, imitated all his movements with a strict exactitude. These improvised gymnasts, with their firm set mouths, worked as methodically as a band of riflemen on parade.

Another entertainment was announced for this evening. I was not present, for the same amusement, night after night, only wearied me. A new paper, a rival of the *Ocean Times*, was to be the great attraction.

I passed the first hours of the night on deck; the sea heaved, and gave warning of stormy weather, and although the sky was perfectly serene, the rolling grew more emphasized. Lying on a seat of the upper deck, I could admire the host of constellations with which the firmament was bespangled, and although there are only 5000 stars, in the whole extent of the celestial sphere, which are visible to the naked eye, this evening I thought I could see millions. There, along the horizon, trailed the tail of Pegasus, in all its zodiacal magnificence, like the starry robe of the queen of fairies. The Peliades ascended the celestial heights with Gemini, who, in spite of their name, do not rise one after the other, like the heroes of the fable. Taurus looked down on me with his great fiery eye, whilst Vega, our future polar-star, shone brilliantly, high up in the azure vault, and not far from her was the circle of diamonds, which form the constellation of Corona Borealis. All these stationary constellations seemed to move with the pitching of the vessel, and in one lurch I saw the mainmast describe a distinct arc of a circle from *ß,* in the Great Bear, to Altair in the Eagle, whilst the moon, already low in the heavens, dipped her crescent in the horizon.

CHAPTER XXIV

The night was stormy, the steam-ship, beaten by the waves, rolled frightfully, without being disabled; the furniture was knocked about with loud crashes, and the crockery began its clatter again. The wind had evidently freshened, and besides this the *Great Eastern* was now in those coasts where the sea is always rough.

At six o'clock in the morning I dragged myself to the staircase, leading on to the upper decks. By clutching at the balusters, and taking advantage of a lurch or two, I succeeded in climbing the steps, and with some difficulty managed to reach the poop. The place was deserted, if one may so speak of a place where was Dr. Pitferge. The worthy man, with his back rounded as a protection against the wind, was leaning against the railing, with his right leg wound tightly round one of the rails. He beckoned for me to go to him-with his head, of course, for he could not spare his hands, which held him up against the violence of the tempest. After several queer movements, twisting myself about like an eel, I reached the upperdeck, where I buttressed myself, after the doctor's fashion.

"We are in for it!" cried he to me; "this will last." Heigh ho! This *Great Eastern*! Just at the moment of arrival, a cyclone, a veritable cyclone is provided on purpose for her."

The Doctor spoke in broken sentences, for the wind cut short his words, but I understood him; the word cyclone carried its explanation with it.

It is well known that these whirlwinds, called hurricanes in the Indian and Atlantic Oceans, tornadoes on the coast of Africa, simoons in the desert, and typhoons in the Chinese Sea, are tempests of such formidable power, that they imperil the largest ships. .

Now the *Great Eastern* was caught in a cyclone. How would this giant make head against it?

"Harm will come to her," repeated Dean Pitferge. "Look, how she dives into the billows."

This was, indeed, the exact position of the steam-ship, whose bows disappeared beneath the mountains of waves, which swept violently against her. It was not possible to see to any distance: there were all the symptoms of a storm, which broke forth in its fury about seven o'clock. The ocean heaved terrifically, the small undulations between the large waves entirely disappeared under an overwhelming wind, the foam-crested billows clashed together, in the wildest uproar, every moment; the waves grew higher, and the *Great Eastern,* cutting through them, pitched frightfully.

"There are but two courses now to choose from," said the Doctor, with the self-possession of a seaman, "either to put the ship's head on to the waves, working with a minimum speed, or take flight and give up the struggle with this baffling sea; but Captain Anderson will do neither one thing nor the other."

"And why not?" I asked.

" Because-" replied the doctor, " because something must happen."

Turning round, I saw the Captain, the first officer, and the chief engineer, muffled in their macintoshes, and clutching at the railings of the bridge; they were enveloped in spray from head to foot. The Captain was smiling as usual, the first officer laughed, and showed his white teeth, at the sight of the ship pitching enough to make one think the masts and chimneys were coming down.

Nevertheless I was really astonished at the Captain's obstinacy. At half past seven, the aspect of the Atlantic was terrible; the sea swept right across the deck at the bows. I watched this grand sight; this struggle between the giant and the billows, and to a certain extent I could sympathize with the Captain's willfulness; but I was forgetting that the power of the sea is infinite, and that nothing made by the hand of man can resist it; and, indeed, powerful as she was, our ship was at last obliged to fly before the tempest.

Suddenly, at about eight o'clock, a violent shock was felt, caused by a formidable swoop of the sea, which struck the ship on her fore larboard quarter.

"That was not a box on the ear, it was a blow in the face," said the Doctor to me.

And the blow had evidently bruised us, for spars appeared on the crests of the waves. Was it part of our ship that was making off in this manner, or the debris of a wreck?

On a sign from the Captain, the *Great Eastern* shifted her course, in order to avoid the spars, which threatened to get entangled in the paddles. Looking more attentively, I saw that the sea had carried away the bulwarks on the port side, which were fifty feet above the surface of the water; the jambs were broken, the taggers torn away, and the shattered remnants of glass still trembled in their casements. The *Great Eastern* had staggered beneath the shock, but she continued her way with an indomitable audacity. It was necessary, as quickly as possible, to remove the spars which encumbered the ship at the bows, and in order to do this it was indispensable to avoid the sea, but the steam-ship obstinately continued to make head against the waves. The spirit of her captain seemed to animate her; he did not want to yield, and yield he would not. An officer and some men were sent to the bows to clear the deck.

" Mind," said the Doctor to me, "the moment of the catastrophe is not far off."

The sailors went towards the bows, whilst we fastened ourselves to the second mast, and looked through the spray, which fell in showers over us with each wave. Suddenly there was another swoop more violent than the first, and the sea poured through the bulwarks by the opened breach, tore off an enormous sheet of cast-iron which covered the bit of the bows, broke away the massive top of the hatchway leading to the crew's berths, and lashing against the starboard bulwarks, swept them away like so much brown paper.

The men were knocked down; one of them, an officer, half-drowned, shook his red whiskers, and picked himself up; then seeing one of the sailors lying unconscious across an anchor, he hurried towards him, lifted him on his shoulders and carried him away. At this moment the rest of the crew escaped through the broken hatchway. There were three feet of water in the tween-decks, new spars covered the sea, and amongst other things several thousand of the dolls, which my countryman had thought to acclimatize in America; these little bodies, torn from their cases by the sea, danced on the summits of the waves, and under less serious circumstances the sight would have been truly ludicrous. In the meantime the inundation was gaining on us, large bodies of water were pouring in through the opened gaps, and according to the engineer, the *Great Eastern* shipped more than two thousand tons of water, enough to float a frigate of the largest size.

"Well!" exclaimed the Doctor, whose hat had been blown off in the hurricane, "to keep in this position is impossible; it is fool-hardy to hold on any longer; we ought to take flight, the steam-ship going with her battered stem ahead, is like a man swimming between two currents, with his mouth open."

This Captain Anderson understood at last, for I saw him run to the little wheel on the bridge which commanded the movement of the rudder, the steam immediately rushed into the cylinders at the stern, and the giant turning like a canoe made head towards the north, and fled before the storm.

At this moment, the Captain, generally so calm and selfpossessed, cried angrily,-

"My ship is disgraced."

CHAPTER XXV

Scarcely had the *Great Eastern* tacked and presented her stern to the waves, than the pitching gave way to perfect steadiness; breakfast was served, and the greater part of the passengers, reassured by the ship's stillness, carrie into the dining-rooms, and took their repast without fear of another shock. Not a plate fell off the table, and not a glass emptied its contents on to the cloth, although the racks had not even been put up. But three quarters of an hour later the furniture was set in motion again, and the crockery clattered together on the pantry shelves, for the *Great Eastern* had resumed her westerly course, which for the time had been interrupted.

I went on deck again with Dr. Pitferge, who seeing the man belonging to the dolls said to him;-

“Your little people have been put to a severe test, sir; those poor babies will never prattle in the United States."

"Pshaw!" replied the enterprising Parisian, " the stock was insured, and my secret has not perished with it."

It was evident my countryman was not a man to be easily disheartened, he bowed to us with a pleasant smile, and we continued our way to the stem, where a steersman told. us that the rudder-chains had been jammed in the interval between the two swoops.

“If that accident had happened when we were turning," said Pitferge to me, "I cannot say what would have become of us, for the sea would have rushed in, in overwhelming torrents; the steam pumps have already begun to reduce the water, but there is more coming yet."

"And what of the unfortunate sailor ?" asked I of the Doctor.

"He is severely wounded on his head, poor fellow! He is a young married fisherman, the father of two children, and this is his first voyage. The Doctor seems to think there is hope of his recovery, and that is what makes me fear for him, but we shall soon see for ourselves. A report was spread that several men had been washed overboard; but happily there was no. foundation for it."

"We have resumed our course at last," said I.

"Yes," replied the Doctor, "the westerly course, against wind and tide, there is no doubt about that," added he; catching hold of a stanchion to prevent himself from rolling on the deck. Do you know what I should do with the *Great Eastern* if she belonged to me? No. Well, I would make a pleasure-boat of her, and charge 10,000 francs a head; there would only be millionnaires on board, and people who were not pressed for time. I would take a month or six weeks going from England to America; the ship never against the waves, and the wind always ahead or astern; there should be no rolling, no pitching, and I would pay a 100L. in any case of sea-sickness."

"That is a practical idea," said I.

"Yes," replied Pitferge, "there's money to be gained or lost by that!"

In the meantime the *Great Eastern* was slowly but steadily continuing her way; the swell was frightful, but her straight stem cut the waves regularly, and shipped no more water. It was no longer a metal mountain making against a mountain of water, but as sedentary as a rock the *Great Eastern* received the billows with perfect indifference. The rain fell in torrents, and we were obliged to take refuge under the eaves of the grand saloon; with the shower the violence of the wind and sea abated; the western sky grew clear, and the last black clouds vanished in the opposite horizon; at ten o'clock the hurricane sent us a farewell gust.

At noon an observation was able to be made and was as follows:-

Lat. 49° 50', N.

Long. 61° 57', W.

Course, 193 miles.

This considerable diminution in the ship's speed could only be attributed to the tempest, which during the night and morning had incessantly beaten against the ship, and a tempest so terrible that one of the passengers, almost an inhabitant of the Atlantic, which he had crossed forty-four times, declared he had never seen the like. The engineer even said that during the storm, when the *Great Eastern* was three days in the trough of the sea, the ship had never been attacked with such violence, and it must be repeated that even if this admirable steam-ship did go at an inferior speed, and rolled decidedly too much, she nevertheless presented a sure security against the fury of the sea, which she resisted like a block, owing to the perfect homogenity of her construction.

But let me also say, however powerful she might be, it was not right to expose her, without any reason whatever, to such heavy seas; for however strong, however imposing a ship may appear, it is not " disgraced" because it flies before the tempest. A commander ought always to remember that a man's life is worth more than the mere satisfaction of his own pride. In any case, to be obstinate is blameable, and to be willful is dangerous. A recent incident in which a dreadful catastrophe happened to a Transatlantic steamer shows us that a captain ought not to struggle blindly against the sea, even when he sees the boat of a rival company creeping ahead.

CHAPTER XXVI

In the meantime the pumps were exhausting the lake which had been formed in the hold of the *Great Eastern,* like a lagoon in the middle of an island; powerfully and rapidly worked by steam they speedily restored to the Atlantic that which belonged to it. The rain had ceased and the wind freshened again, but the sky, swept by the tempest, was clear. I stayed several hours after dark walking on deck. Great floods of light poured from the half-opened hatchways of the saloons, and at the stern stretched a phosphorescent light as far as the eye could reach, streaked here and there by the luminous crests of the waves. The stars reflected in the lactescent water appeared and disappeared, as though peering through rapidly driving clouds. Night had spread her sombre covering far and near; forward roared the thunder of the wheels, whilst beneath me I heard the clanking of the rudder-chains.

Going back to the saloon door I was surprised to see there a compact crowd of spectators, and to hear vociferous applauses, for, in spite of the day's disasters, the entertainment was taking place as usual. Not a thought of the wounded and, perhaps, dying sailor. The assembly seemed highly animated, and loud hurrahs hailed the appearance of a troop of minstrels on board the *Great Eastern*. The niggers-black, or blackened, according to their origin-were no others than sailors in disguise. They were dressed in cast-off trumpery, ornamented with sea-biscuits for buttons; the opera-glasses which they sported were composed of two bottles fastened together, and their jew's-harps consisted of catgut stretched on cork. These merry- andrews were amusing enough upon the whole; they sang comic songs, and improvised a mixture of puns and cock-and-bull stories. The uproarious cheers with which their performances were greeted only made them increase their contortions and grimaces, until one of them, as nimble as a monkey, finished the performance by dancing the sailor's hornpipe.

However amusing the minstrels may have been, they had not succeeded in attracting all the passengers. Numbers of them had flocked to their usual haunt, the "smoking-room," and were eagerly pressing round the gaming-tables, where enormous stakes were being made, some defending their acquisitions during the voyage, others trying to conquer fate by making rash wagers at the last moment. The room was in a violent uproar, one could hear the voice of the money agent crying the stakes, the oaths of the losers, the clinking of gold, and the rustling of dollar-papers; then there was a sudden lull, the uproar was silenced by a bold stake, but as soon as the result was known the noise was redoubled.

I very seldom entered the smoking-room, for I have a horror of gambling. It is always a vulgar and often an unhealthy pastime, and it is a vice which does not go alone; the man who gambles will find himself capable of any evil. Here reigned Harry Drake in the midst of his parasites, here also flourished those adventurers who were going to seek their fortunes in America. I always avoided a meeting with these boisterous men, so this evening I passed the door without going in, when my attention was arrested by a violent outburst of cries and curses. I listened, and, after a moment's silence, to my great astonishment I thought could distinguish Fabian's voice. What could he be doing in this place? Had he come here to look for his enemy, and thus the catastrophe, until now avoided, been brought about?

I quickly pushed the door open: at this moment the uproar was at its height. In the midst of the crowd of gamblers I saw Fabian standing facing Harry Drake. I hurried towards him, Harry Drake had undoubtedly grossly insulted him, for Fabian was aiming a blow with his fist at him, and if it did not reach the place it was intended for, it was only because Corsican suddenly appeared and stopped him with a quick gesture.

But, addressing himself to his enemy, Fabian said, in a cold, sarcastic tone,-

"Do you accept that blow?"

"Yes," replied Drake, "and here is my card!"

Thus, in spite of our efforts, an inevitable fatality had brought these two deadly enemies together. It was too late to separate them now, events must take their course. Captain Corsican looked at me, and I was surprised to see sadness rather than annoyance in his eyes.

In the meantime Fabian picked up the card which Harry Drake had thrown on the table; He held it between the tips of his fingers as if loath to touch it. Corsican was pale, and my heart beat wildly. At first Fabian looked at the card, and read the name on it, then with a voice stifled by passion he cried,-

" Harry. Drake! You! You! You!"

"The same, Captain Mac Elwin," quietly replied Fabian's rival.

We were not deceived, if Fabian was ignorant until now of Drake's name, the latter was. only too well aware of Fabian's presence on the *Great Eastern*.

CHAPTER XXVII

The next day, at break of dawn, I went in search of Captain Corsican, whom I found in the grand saloon. He had passed the night with Fabian, who was still suffering from the shock which the name of Ellen's husband had given him. Did a secret intuition tell him that Drake was not alone on board? Had Ellen's presence been revealed to him by the appearance of this man? Lastly, could he guess that the poor crazed woman was the young girl whom he so fondly loved? Corsican could not say, for Fabian had not uttered one word all night

Corsican resented Fabian's wrongs with a kind of brotherly feeling. The intrepid nature of the latter had from childhood irresistibly attracted him, and he was now in the greatest despair.

"I came in too late," said he to me. "Before Fabian could have raised his hand, I ought to have struck that wretch."

"Useless violence," replied I. "Harry Drake would not have risked a quarrel with you; he has a grudge against Fabian, and a meeting between the two had become inevitable."

"You are right," said the Captain. "That rascal has got what he wanted; he knew Fabian, his past life, and his love. Perhaps Ellen, deprived of reason, betrayed her secret thoughts, or, rather, did not Drake before his marriage learn from the loyal young woman all he was ignorant of regarding her past life? Urged by a base impulse, and finding himself in contact with Fabian, he has waited for an opportunity in which he could assume the part of the offended. This scoundrel ought to be a clever duelist"

"Yes," replied I. "He has already had three or four encounters of the kind."

"My dear sir," said the Captain, "it is not the duel in itself which I fear for Fabian. Captain McElwin is one of those who never trouble themselves about danger, but it is the result of this engagement which is to be dreaded. If Fabian were to kill this man, however vile he may be, it would place an impossible barrier between Ellen and himself, and Heaven knows, the unhappy woman needs a support, like Fabian, in the state she now is."

"True," said I; "whatever happens we can but hope that Harry Drake will fall. Justice is on our side."

"Certainly," replied the Captain, "but one cannot help feeling distressed to think that even at the risk of my own life I could not have spared Fabian this."

"Captain," said I, taking the hand of this devoted friend, "Drake has not sent his seconds yet, so that, although circumstances are against us, I do not despair."

"Do you know any means of preventing the duel?"

"None at present; at the same time, if the meeting must take place, it seems to me that it can only do so in America, and before we get there, chance, which has brought about this state of things, will, perhaps, turn the scales in our favour."

Captain Corsican shook his head like a man who had no faith in the efficacy of chance in human affairs. At this moment Fabian went up the stairs leading to the deck. I only saw him for a moment, but I was struck by the deadly pallor of his face. The wound had been reopened, and it was sad to see him wandering aimlessly about, trying to avoid us.

Even friendship may be troublesome at times, and Corsican and I thought it better to respect his grief rather than interfere with him. But suddenly Fabian turned, and coming towards us, said,-

"The mad woman, was she! It was Ellen, was it not? Poor Ellen!"

He was still doubtful, and went away without waiting for an answer, which we had not the courage to give.

CHAPTER XXVIII

At noon, Drake had not sent Fabian his seconds to my knowledge, and these were preliminaries which could not be dispensed with, if Drake determined to demand immediate satisfaction. Might we not take hope from this delay? I knew that the Saxon race do not regard a debt of honour as we do, and that duels had almost disappeared from English customs, for, as I have already said, not only is there a severe law against duelists, but, moreover, the public opinion is strongly averse to them. At the same time, in this, which was an uncommon case, the engagement had evidently been voluntarily sought for; the offended had, so to speak, provoked the offender, and my reasonings always tended to the same conclusion, that a meeting between Fabian and Harry Drake was inevitable.

The deck was at this moment crowded with passengers and crew returning from service.

At half-past twelve the observation resulted in the following note :-

Lat 40° 33′ N.

Long. 66° 24 W.

Course, 214 miles.

Thus the *Great Eastern* was only 348 miles from Sandy Hook Point, a narrow tongue of land which forms the entrance to the New York harbour; it would not be long before we were in American seas.

I did not see Fabian in his usual place at lunch, but Drake was there, and although talkative, he did not appear to be quite at his ease. Was he trying to drown his fears in wine? I cannot say, but he indulged in bountiful libations with his friends. Several times I saw him leering at me, but insolent as he was, he dared not look me in the face. Was he looking for Fabian among the crowd of guests? I noticed he left the table abruptly before the meal was finished,and I got up immediately, in order to observe him, but he went to his cabin and shut himself up there.

I went up on deck. Not a wave disturbed the calm surface of the sea, and the sky was unsullied by a cloud; the two mirrors mutually reflected their azure hue. I met Doctor Pitferge, who gave me bad news of the wounded sailor. The invalid was getting worse, and, in spite of the doctor's assurance, it was difficult to think that he could recover.

At four o'clock, a few minutes before dinner, a ship was hailed to larboard. The first officer told me he thought it must be the *City of Paris*, one of the finest steamers of the *Inman Company*, but he was mistaken, for the steamer coming nearer, sent us her name, which was the *Saxonia*, belonging to the *National Steamship Company*. For a few minutes the two boats came alongside, within two or three cables' length of each other. The deck of the *Saxonia* was covered with passengers, who saluted us with loud cheers.

At five o'clock another ship on the horizon, but too far off for her nationality to be recognized. This time it was undoubtedly the *City of Paris*. This meeting with ships, and the salutation between the Atlantic's visitors, caused great excitement on board. One can understand that as there is little difference between one ship and another, the common danger of facing the uncertain element unites even strangers by a friendly bond.

At six o'clock a third ship appeared, the *Philadelphia*, one of the Inman line, used for the transportation of emigrants from Liverpool to New York. We were evidently in frequented seas, and land could not be far off. How I longed to reach it! The *Europe*, a steamer belonging to the *Transatlantic Company*, carrying passengers from Havre to New York, was expected, but she did not come in sight, and had most likely taken a more northerly course.

Night closed in about half-past seven. As the sun sank below the horizon, the moon grew brighter and for some time hung shining in the heavens. A prayer-meeting, held by Captain Anderson, interspersed with hymns, lasted until nine o'clock.

The day passed without either Captain Corsican or myself receiving a visit from Drake's second.

CHAPTER XXIX

The next day, Monday, the 8th of April, the weather was very fine. I found the Doctor on deck basking in the sun. He came up to me. "Ah well!" said he, "our poor sufferer died in the night. The doctor never gave him up-oh, those doctors! They never will give in. This is the fourth man we have lost since we left Liverpool, the fourth gone towards paying the *Great Eastern's* debt, and we are not at the end of our voyage yet."

"Poor fellow," said I, "just as we are nearing port, and the American coast almost in sight. What will become of his widow and little children?"

"Would you have it otherwise, my dear sir. It is the law, the great law! We must die! We must give way to others. It is my opinion we die simply because we are occupying a place which by rights belongs to another. Now can you tell me how many people will have died during my existence if I live to be sixty?"

"I have no idea, Doctor."

"The calculation is simple enough," resumed Dean Pitferge. "If I live sixty years, I shall have been in the world 21,900 days, or 525,600 hours, or 31,536,000 minutes, or lastly, 1,892,160,000 seconds, in round numbers 2,000,000,000 seconds. Now in that time two thousand millions individuals who were in the way of their successors will have died, and when I have become inconvenient, I shall be put out of the way in the same manner, so that the long and short of the matter is to put off becoming inconvenient as long as possible."

The Doctor continued for some time arguing on this subject, tending to prove to me a very simple theory, the mortality of human creatures. I did not think it worth while to discuss the point with him, so I let him have his say. Whilst we paced backwards and forwards, the Doctor talking, and I listening, I noticed that the carpenters on board were busy repairing the battered stem. If Captain Anderson did not wish to arrive in New York with damages, the carpenters would have to hurry over their work, for the *Great Eastern* was rapidly speeding through the tranquil waters; this I understood from the lively demeanour of the young lovers, who no longer thought of counting the turns of the wheels. The long pistons expanded, and the enormous cylinders heaving on their axle-swings, looked like a great peal of bells clanging together at random. The wheels made eleven revolutions a minute, and the steam-ship went at the rate of thirteen miles an hour.

At noon the officers dispensed with making an observation; they knew their situation by calculation, and land must be signaled before long.

While I was walking on deck after lunch, Captain Corsican came up. I saw, from the thoughtful expression on his face, that he had something to tell me.

"Fabian," said he, "has received Drake's seconds. I am to be his second, and he begs me to ask you if you would kindly be present on the occasion. He may rely on you?"

"Yes, Captain; so all hope of deferring or preventing this meeting has vanished?"

"All hope."

"But tell me, how did the quarrel arise?"

"A discussion about the play was a pretext for it, nothing else. The fact is if Fabian was not aware who Harry Drake was, it is quite evident he knew Fabian, and the name of Fabian is so odious to him that he would gladly slay the man to whom it belongs."

"Who are Drake's seconds?" I asked.

"One of them is that actor-"

"Doctor T--?"

"Just so; the other is a Yankee I do not know."

"When are you to expect them?"

"I am waiting for them here."

And just as he spoke I saw the seconds coming towards us. Doctor T-- cleared his throat; he undoubtedly thought a great deal more of himself as the representative of a rogue. His companion, another of Drake's associates, was one of those extraordinary merchants who has always for sale anything you may ask him to buy.

Doctor T-- spoke first, after making a very emphatic bow, which Captain Corsican hardly condescended to acknowledge.

"Gentlemen," said Doctor T--, in a grave tone, "our friend Drake, a gentleman whose merit and deportment cannot fail to be appreciated by every one, has sent us to arrange a somewhat delicate affair with you; that is to say, Captain Fabian Mac Elwin, to whom we first addressed ourselves, referred us to you as his representative. I hope that we shall be able to come to an understanding between ourselves worthy the position of gentlemen touching the delicate object of our mission."

We made no reply, but allowed the gentleman to become embarrassed with his delicacy.

"Gentlemen," continued he, " there is not the remotest doubt but that Captain Mac Elwin is in the wrong. That gentleman has unreasonably, and without the slightest pretext, questioned the honour of Harry Drake's proceedings in a matter of play, and without any provocation offered him the greatest insult a gentleman could receive."

These honeyed words made the Captain impatient, he bit his moustache, and could refrain speaking no longer.

"Come to the point," said he sharply to Doctor T--, whose speech he had interrupted, "we don't want so many words; the affair is simple enough; Captain Mac Elwin raised his hand against Mr. Drake, your friend accepted the blow, he assumes the part of the offended, and demands satisfaction. He has the choice of arms. What next?"

"Does Captain Mac Elwin accept the challenge?" asked the Doctor, baffled by Corsican's tone.

"Decidedly."

"Our friend, Harry Drake, has chosen swords."

"Very well, and where is the engagement to take place? In New York?"

"No, here on board."

"On board, be it so; at what time? Tomorrow morning?"

"This evening at six o'clock, at the end of the upperdeck, which will be deserted at that time."

"Very well."

Thus saying, the Captain took my arm, and turned his back on Dr. T--.

CHAPTER XXX

It was no longer possible to put off the duel. Only a few hours separated us from the moment when Fabian and Harry Drake must meet. What could be the reason of this haste? How was it that Harry Drake had not delayed the duel until he and his enemy had disembarked? Was it because this ship, freighted by a French company, seemed to him the most favourable ground for a meeting which must be a deadly struggle? Or rather, might not Drake have a secret interest in freeing himself of Fabian before the latter could set foot on the American continent, or suspect the presence of Ellen on board, which he must have thought was unknown to all save himself? Yes, it must have been for this reason.

"Little matter, after all," said the Captain; "far better to have it over."

"Shall I ask Dr. Pitferge to be present at the duel as a doctor?"

"Yes, it would be well to do so."

Corsican left me to go to Fabian. At this moment the bell on deck began tolling, and when I inquired of a helmsman the reason of this unusual occurrence, he told me that it was for the .burial of the sailor who had died in the night, and that the sad ceremony was about to take place. The sky, until now so clear, became overcast, and dark clouds loomed threateningly in the south.

At the sound of the bell the passengers flocked to the starboard side. The bridges, paddle-boards, bulwarks, masts and ship's boats, hanging from their davits, were crowded with spectators, the officers, sailors, and stokers off duty, stood in ranks on deck. At two o'clock a group of sailors appeared at the far end of the upper deck, they had left the hospital, and were passing the rudder-engine. The corpse, sewn in a piece of sail and stretched on a board, with a cannon ball at the feet, was carried by four men. The body, covered with the British flag, and followed by the dead man's comrades, slowly advanced into the midst of the spectators, who uncovered their heads as the procession passed.

On their arrival at the starboard paddle-wheel, the corpse was deposited on a landing of a staircase which terminated at the main deck.

In front of the row of spectators, standing one above the other, were Captain Anderson and his principal officers in full uniform. The

Captain, holding a prayer-book in his hand, took his hat off, and for some minutes, during a profound silence, which not even the breeze interrupted, he solemnly read the prayer for the dead, every word of which was distinctly audible in the deathlike silence.

On a sign from the Captain the body, released by the bearers, sank into the sea. For one moment it floated on the surface, became upright, and then disappeared in a circle of foam.

At this moment the voice of the sailor on watch was heard crying " Land!"

CHAPTER XXXI

The land announced at the moment when the sea was closing over the corpse of the poor sailor was low-lying and of a yellow colour. This line of slightly elevated downs was Long Island, a great sandy bank enlivened with vegetation, which stretches along the American coast from Montauk Point to Brooklyn, adjoining New York. Several yachts were coasting along this island, which is covered with villas and pleasure-houses, the favourite resorts of the New Yorkists.

Every passenger waved his hand to the land so longed for after the tedious voyage, which had not been exempt from painful accidents. Every telescope was directed towards this first specimen of the American continent, and each saw it under a different aspect. The Yankee beheld in it his mother-land; the Southerner regarded these northern lands with a kind of scorn, the scorn of the conquered for the conqueror; the Canadian looked upon it as a man who had only one step to take to call himself a citizen of the Union; the Californian in his mind's eye traversed the plains of the Far West, and crossing the Rocky Mountains had already set foot on their inexhaustible mines. The Mormonite, with elevated brow and scornful lip, hardly noticed these shores, but peered beyond to where stood the City of the Saints on the borders of Salt Lake, in the far off deserts. As for the young lovers, this continent was to them the Promised Land.

In the meanwhile the sky was growing more and more threatening. A dark line of clouds gathered in the zenith, and a suffocating heat penetrated the atmosphere as though a July sun was shining directly above us.

"Would you like me to astonish you?" said the Doctor, who had joined me on the gangway.

"Astonish me, Doctor?"

"Well, then, we shall have a storm, perhaps a thunderstorm, before the day is over."

"A thunder-storm in the month of April!" I cried.

"The *Great Eastern* does not trouble herself about seasons," replied Dean Pitferge, shrugging his shoulders. "It is a tempest called forth expressly on her account. Look at the threatening aspect of those clouds which cover the sky; they look like antediluvian animals, and before long they will devour each other."

"I confess," said I, "the sky looks stormy, and were it three months later I should be of your opinion, but not at this time of year."

"I tell you," replied the Doctor, growing animated, "the storm will burst out before many hours are past I feel it like a barometer. Look at those vapours rising in a mass, observe that cirrus, those mares' tails which are blending together, and those thick circles which surround the horizon. Soon there will be a rapid condensing of vapour, which will consequently produce electricity. Besides the mercury has suddenly fallen, and the prevailing wind is south-west, the only one which can brew a storm in winter."

"Your observations may be very true, Doctor," said I, not willing to yield, "but who has ever witnessed a thunder-storm at this season, and in this latitude?"

"We have proof, sir, we have proof on record. Mild winters are often marked by storms. You ought only to have lived in 1172, or even in 1824, and you would have heard the roaring of the thunder, in the first instance in February, and in the second in December. In the month of January, 1837, a thunder-bolt fell near Drammen in Norway, and did considerable mischief. Last year, in the month of February, fishing-smacks from Treport were struck by lightning. If I had time to consult statistics I would soon put you to silence."

"Well, Doctor, since you will have it so, we shall soon see. At any rate, you are not afraid of thunder?"

"Not I," replied the Doctor. "The thunder is my friend; better still, it is my doctor."

"Your doctor? "

"Most certainly. I was struck by lightning in my bed on the 13th July, 1857, at Kew, near London, and it cured me of paralysis in my right arm, when the doctors had given up the case as hopeless."

"You must be joking."

"Not at all. It is an economical treatment by electricity. My dear sir, there are many very authentic facts which prove that thunder surpasses the most skilful physicians, and its intervention is truly marvelous in apparently hopeless cases."

"Nevertheless," said I, "I have little trust in your doctor, and would not willingly consult him."

"Because you have never seen him at work. Stay; here is an instance which I have heard of as occurring in 1817. A peasant in Connecticut, who was suffering from asthma, supposed to be incurable, was struck by lightning in a field, and radically cured."

In fact I believe the Doctor would have been capable of making the thunder into pills.

"Laugh, ignoramus!" said he to me. "You know nothing either of the weather or medicine !"

CHAPTER XXXII

Dean Pitferge left me, but I remained on deck, watching the storm rise. Corsican was still closeted with Fabian, who was undoubtedly making some arrangements in case of misfortune. I then remembered that he had a sister in New York, and I shuddered at the thought that perhaps we should have to carry to her the news of her brother's death. I should like to have seen Fabian, but I thought it better not to disturb either him or Captain Corsica.

At four o'clock we came in sight of land stretching before Long Island. It was Fire Island. In the center rose a lighthouse, which shone over the surrounding land. The passengers again invaded the upper decks and bridges. All eyes were strained towards the coast, distant about six miles. They were waiting for the moment when the arrival of the pilot should settle the great pool business. It may be thought that those who had night quarters, and I was of the number, had given up all pretensions, and that those with the day quarters, except those included between four and six o'clock, had no longer any chance. Before night the pilot would come on board and settle this affair, so that all the interest was now concentrated in the seven or eight persons to whom fate had attributed the next quarters. The latter were taking advantage of their good luck-selling, buying, and reselling their chances, bartering with such energy one might almost have fancied oneself in the Royal Exchange.

At sixteen minutes past four a small schooner, bearing towards the steam-ship, was signaled to starboard. There was no longer any possible doubt of its being the pilot's boat, and he would be on board in fourteen or fifteen minutes at the most; The struggle was now between the possessors of the second and third quarters from four to five o'clock. Demands and offers were made with renewed vivacity. Then absurd wagers were laid even on the pilot's person, the tenor of which I have faithfully given.

"Ten dollars that the pilot is married."

"Twenty that he is a widower."

"Thirty dollars that he has a moustache."

"Sixty that he has a wart on his nose."

"A hundred dollars that he will step on board with his right foot first."

"He will smoke."

"He will have a pipe in his mouth."

"No! A cigar."

"No!" "Yes!" "No!"

And twenty other wagers quite as ridiculous, which found those more absurd still to accept them.

In the meanwhile the little schooner was sensibly approaching the steam-ship, and we could distinguish her graceful proportions. These charming little pilot-boats, of about fifty or sixty tons, are good sea-boats, skimming over the water like sea-gulls. The schooner, gracefully inclined, was bearing windward in spite of the breeze, which had begun to freshen. Her mast and foresails stood out clearly against the dark background of clouds, and the sea foamed beneath her bows. When at two cables' length from the *Great Eastern,* she suddenly veered and launched a ship's boat. Captain Anderson gave orders to heave-to, and for the first time during a fortnight the wheels of the screw were motionless. A man got into the boat, which four sailors quickly pulled to the steam-ship. A rope ladder was thrown over the side of the giant down to the pilot in his little nutshell, which the latter caught, and, skillfully climbing, sprang on deck.

He was received with joyous cries by the winners, and exclamations of disappointment from the losers. The pool was regulated by the following statements :-

"The pilot was married."

"He had no wart on his nose."

"He had a light moustache."

"He had jumped on board. With both feet."

"Lastly, it was thirty-six minutes past four o'clock when he set foot on the deck of the *Great Eastern*."

The possessor of the thirty-third quarter thus gained the ninety-six dollars, and it was Captain Corsican, who had hardly thought of the unexpected gain. It was not long before he appeared on deck, and when the pool was presented to him, he begged Captain Anderson to keep it for the widow of the young sailor whose death had been caused by the inroad of the sea. The Captain shook his hand without saying a word, but a moment afterwards a sailor came up to Corsican, and, bowing awkwardly, " Sir," said he, "my mates have sent me to say that you are a very kind gentleman, and they all thank you in the name of poor Wilson, who cannot thank you for himself."

The Captain, moved by the rough sailor's speech, silently pressed his hand.

As for the pilot, he was a man of short stature, with not much of the sailor-look about him. He wore a glazed hat, black trousers, a brown overcoat lined with red, and carried an umbrella. He was master on board now.

In springing on deck, before he went to the bridge, he had thrown a bundle of papers among the passengers, who eagerly pounced on them. They were European and American journals-the political and civil bonds which again united the *Great Eastern* to the two continents.

CHAPTER XXXIII

The storm was gathering, and a black arch of clouds had formed over our heads; the atmosphere was misty; nature was evidently about to justify Dr. Pitferge's presentiments. The steam-ship had slackened her speed, and the wheels only made three or four revolutions a minute; volumes of white steam escaped from the half-open valves, the anchor-chains were cleared, and the British flag floated from the mainmast; these arrangements Captain Anderson had made preparatory to mooring. The pilot, standing on the top of the starboard paddle, guided the steam-ship through the narrow passages; but the tide was already turning, so that the *Great Eastern* could not yet cross the bar of the Hudson, and we must wait till next day.

At a quarter to five by the pilot's order the anchors were let go; the chains rattled through the hawse-holes with a noise like thunder. I even thought for a moment that the storm had burst forth. When the anchors were firmly embedded in the sand, the *Great Eastern* swung round by the ebb tide, remained motionless, and not a wave disturbed the surface of the water.

At this moment the steward's trumpet sounded for the last time; it called the passengers to their farewell dinner. The *Society of Freighters* would be prodigal with the champagne, and no one wished to be absent. An hour later the saloons were crowded with guests, and the deck deserted.

However, seven persons left their places unoccupied; the two adversaries, who were going to stake their lives in a duel, the four seconds, and the Doctor, who was to be present at the engagement. The time and the place for the meeting had been well chosen; there was not a creature on deck; the passengers were in the dining-rooms, the sailors in their berths, the officers absorbed with their own particular bottles, and not a steersman on board, for the ship was motionless at anchor.

At ten minutes past five the Doctor and I were joined by Fabian and Captain Corsican. I had not seen Fabian since the scene in the smoking-room. He seemed to me sad, but very calm. The thought of the duel troubled him little, apparently; his mind was elsewhere, and his eyes wandered restlessly in search of Ellen. He held out his hand to me without saying a word.

"Has not Harry Drake arrived!" asked the Captain of me.

"Not yet," I replied.

"Let us go to the stern; that is the place of rendezvous."

Fabian, Captain Corsican, and I, walked along the upper decks; the sky was growing dark; we heard the distant roar of thunder rumbling along the horizon. It was like a monotonous bass, enlivened by the hips and hurrahs issuing from the saloons; flashes of lightning darted through the black clouds, and the atmosphere was powerfully charged with electricity.

At twenty minutes past five Harry Drake and his seconds made their appearance. The gentlemen bowed to us, which honour we strictly returned. Drake did not utter a word, but his face showed signs of ill-concealed excitement. He cast a look of malignant hatred on Fabian; but the latter, leaning against the hatchway, did not even see him; so absorbed was he in a profound meditation, he seemed not yet to have thought of the part he was to play in this drama.

In the meanwhile Captain Corsican, addressing himself to the Yankee, one of Drake's seconds, asked him for the swords, which the latter presented to him. They were battle swords, the basket-hilts of which entirely protected the hand which held them. Corsican took them, bent, and measured them, and then allowed the Yankee to choose. Whilst these preparations were being made, Harry Drake had taken off his hat and jacket, unbuttoned his shirt, and turned up his sleeves; then he seized his sword, and I saw that he was left-handed, which gave him, accustomed to right-handed antagonists, an unquestionable advantage.

Fabian had not yet left the place where he was standing. One would have thought that these preparations had nothing to do with him. Captain Corsican went up to him, touched him, and showed him the sword. Fabian looked at the glittering steel, and it seemed as if his memory came back to him at that moment. He grasped his sword with a firm hand.

"Right!"He murmured; "I remember!"

Then he placed himself opposite Harry Drake, who immediately assumed the defensive.

"Proceed, gentlemen," said the Captain.

They immediately crossed swords. From the first clashing of steel, several rapid passes on both sides, certain extrications, parries, and thrusts proved to me the equality in strength of the opponents. I augured well for Fabian. He was cool, self-possessed, and almost indifferent to the struggle; certainly less affected by it than were his own seconds. Harry Drake, on the contrary, scowled at him with flashing eyes and clenched teeth, his head bent forward, and his whole countenance indicative of a hatred which deprived him of all composure. He had come there to kill, and kill he would.

After the first engagement, which lasted some minutes, swords were lowered. With the exception of a slight scratch on Fabian's arm, neither of the combatants had been wounded. They rested, and Drake wiped off the perspiration with which his face was bathed.

The storm now burst forth in all its fury. The thunder was continuous, and broke out in loud deafening reports; the atmosphere was charged with electricity to such an extent that the swords were gilded with luminous crests, like lightning conductors in the midst of thunder clouds.

After a few moments' rest, Corsican again gave the signal to proceed, and Fabian and Harry Drake again fell to work.

This time the fight was much more animated; Fabian defending himself with astounding calmness, Drake madly attacking him. Several times I expected a stroke from Fabian, which was not even attempted.

Suddenly, after some quick passes, Drake made a rapid stroke. I thought that Fabian must have been struck in the chest, but, warding off the blow, he struck Harry Drake's sword smartly. The latter raised and covered himself by a swift semi-circle; whilst the lightning rent the clouds overhead.

Suddenly, and without anything to explain this strange surrender of himself, Fabian dropped his sword. Had he been mortally wounded without our noticing it? The blood rushed wildly to my heart. Fabian's eyes had grown singularly animated.

"Defend yourself," roared Drake, drawing himself up like a tiger ready to spring on to his prey.

I thought that it was all over with Fabian, disarmed as he was. Corsican threw himself between him and his enemy, to prevent the latter from striking a defenceless man; but now Harry Drake in his turn stood motionless.

I turned, and saw Ellen, pale as death, her hands stretched out, coming towards the duelists Fabian, fascinated by this apparition, remained perfectly still.

"You! You!" cried Harry Drake to Ellen; "you here!"

His uplifted blade gleamed as though on fire; one might have said it was the sword of the archangel Michael in the hands of a demon. Suddenly a brilliant flash of lightning lit up the whole stern. I was almost knocked down, and felt suffocated, for the air was filled with sulphur; but by a powerful effort I regained my senses.

I had fallen on one knee, but I got up and looked around. Ellen was leaning on Fabian. Harry Drake seemed petrified, and remained in the same position, but his face had grown black.

Had the unhappy man been struck when attracting the lightning with his blade ?

Ellen left Fabian, and went up to Drake with her face full of holy compassion. She placed her hand on his shoulder; even this light touch was enough to disturb the equilibrium, and Drake fell to the ground a corpse.

Ellen bent over the body, whilst we drew back terrified. The wretched Harry Drake was dead.

"Struck by lightning," said Dean Pitferge, catching hold of my arm. "Struck by lightning! Ah! Will you not now believe in the intervention of thunder?"

Had Harry Drake indeed been struck by lightning as Dean Pitferge affirmed, or rather, as the doctor on board said, had a blood-vessel broken in his chest? I can only say there was nothing now but a corpse before our eyes.

CHAPTER XXXIV

The next day, Tuesday, the 9th of April, the *Great Eastern* weighed anchor, and set sail to enter the Hudson, the pilot guiding her with an unerring eye. The storm had spent itself in the night, and the last black clouds disappeared below the horizon. The aspect of the sea was enlivened by a flotilla of schooners, waiting along the coast for the breeze.

A small steamer came alongside, and we were boarded by the officer of the New York sanitary commissioners. It was not long before we passed the light-boat which marks the channels of the Hudson, and ranged near Sandy Hook Point, where a group of spectators greeted us with a volley of hurrahs. When the *Great Eastern* had gone round the interior bay formed by Sandy Hook Point, through the flotilla of fishing-smacks, I caught a glimpse of the verdant heights of New Jersey, the enormous forts on the bay, then the low line of the great city stretching between the Hudson and East river.

In another hour, after having ranged opposite the New York quays, the *Great Eastern* was moored in the Hudson, and the anchors became entangled in the submarine cable, which must necessarily be broken on her departure.

Then began the disembarkation of all my fellow voyagers whom I should never see again: Californians, Southerners, Mormonites, and the young lovers. I was waiting for Fabian and Corsican.

I had been obliged to inform Captain Anderson of the incidents relating to the duel which had taken place on board. The doctors made their report, and nothing whatever having been found wrong in the death of Harry Drake, orders were given that the last duties might be rendered to him on land.

At this moment Cockburn, the statician, who had not spoken to me the whole of the voyage, came up and said,"Do you know, sir, how many turns the wheels have made during our passage?"

" I do not, sir."

"One hundred thousand, seven hundred and twenty three."

"Ah ! really sir, and the screw?"

"Six hundred and eight thousand, one hundred and thirty."

"I am much obliged to you, sir, for the information."

And the statician left me without any farewell whatever Fabian and Corsican joined me at this moment. Fabian pressed my hand warmly.

" Ellen," said he to me, "Ellen will recover. Her reason came back to her for a moment. Ah! God is just, and He will restore her wholly to us."

Whilst thus speaking, Fabian smiled as he thought of the future. As for Captain Corsican, he kissed me heartily without any ceremony.

"Good-bye, good-bye, we shall see you again," he cried to me, when he had taken his place in the tender where were Fabian and Ellen, under the care of Mrs. R--, Captain Mac Elwin's sister, who had come to meet her brother.

Then the tender sheered off, taking the first convoy of passengers to the Custom House pier.

I watched them as they went farther and farther away, and, seeing Ellen sitting between Fabian and his sister, I could not doubt that care, devotion, and love would restore to this poor mind the reason of which grief had robbed it.

Just then some one took hold of my arm, and I knew it was Dr. Pitferge.

"Well," said he, "and what is going to become of you?"

"My idea was, Doctor, since the *Great Eastern* remains a hundred and ninety-two hours at New York, and as I must return with her, to spend the hundred and ninety two hours in America. Certainly it is but a week, but a week well spent is, perhaps, long enough to see New York, the Hudson, the Mohawk Valley, Lake Erie, Niagara, and all the country made familiar by Cooper.

"Ah! You are going to the Niagara!" cried Dean Pitferge. "I'll declare I should not be sorry to see it again, and if my proposal does not seem very disagreeable to you-"

The worthy Doctor amused me with his crotchets. I had taken a fancy to him, and here was a well-instructed guide placed at my service.

"That's settled, then," said I to him.

A quarter of an hour later we embarked on the tender, and at three o'clock were comfortably lodged in two rooms of Fifth Avenue Hotel.

CHAPTER XXXV

A week to spend in America! The *Great Eastern* was to set sail on the 16th of April, and it was now the 9th, and three o'clock in the afternoon, when I set foot on the land of the Union. A week! There are furious tourists and express travelers who would probably find this time enough to visit the whole of North America; but I had no such pretention, not even to visit New York thoroughly, and to write, after this extra rapid inspection, a book on the manners and customs of the Americans. But the constitution and physical aspect of New York is soon seen; it is hardly more varied than a chess-board. The streets, cut at right angles, are called avenues when they are straight, and streets when irregular. The numbers on the principal thoroughfares are a very practical but monotonous arrangement. American cars run through all the avenues. Any one who has seen one quarter of New York knows the whole of the great city, except, perhaps, that intricacy of streets and confused alleys appropriated by the commercial population.

New York is built on a tongue of land, and all its activity is centered on the end of that tongue; on either side extend the Hudson and East River, arms of the sea, in fact, on which ships are seen and ferry-boats ply, connecting the town on the right hand with Brooklyn, and on the left with the shores of New Jersey.

A single artery intersects the symmetrical quarters of New York, and that is old Broadway, the Strand of London, and the Boulevard Montmatre of Paris; hardly passable at its lower end, where it is crowded with people, and almost deserted higher up; a street where sheds and marble palaces are huddled together; a stream of carriages, omnibusses, cabs, drays, and wagons, with the pavement for its banks, across which a bridge has been thrown for the traffic of foot passengers. Broadway is New York, and it was there that the Doctor and I walked until evening.

After having dined at Fifth Avenue Hotel, I ended my day's work by going to the Barnum Theatre, where they were acting a play called "New York Streets," which attracted a large audience. In the fourth Act there was a fire, and real fire-engines, worked by real firemen; hence the "great attraction."

The next morning I left the Doctor to his own affairs, and agreed to meet him at the hotel at two o'clock. My first proceeding was to go to the Post Office, 51, Liberty Street, to get any letters awaiting me there; then I went to No.2, Bowling Green, at the bottom of Broadway, the residence of the French consul, M. le Baron Gauldnée Boilleau, who received me very kindly. From here I made my way to cash a draft at Hoffman's; lastly, I went to No. 25, Thirty-Sixth Street, where resided Mrs. R--, Fabian's sister. I was impatient to get news of Ellen and my two friends; and here I learnt that, following the Doctor's advice, Mrs. R--, Fabian, and Corsican had left New York, taking with them the young lady, thinking that the air and quiet of the country might have a beneficial effect on her. A line from Captain Corsican informed me of this sudden departure. The kind fellow had been to Fifth Avenue Hotel without meeting me, but he promised to keep me acquainted with their whereabouts. They thought of stopping at the first place that attracted Ellen's attention, and, staying there as long as the charm lasted; he hoped that I should not leave without bidding them a last farewell. Yes, were it but for a few hours, I should be happy to see Ellen, Fabian, and Corsican once again. But such are the drawbacks of traveling, hurried as I was, they gone and I going, each our separate ways, it seemed hardly likely I should see them again.

At two o'clock I returned to the hotel, and found the Doctor in the bar-room, which was full of people. It is a public hall, where travelers and passers-by mingled together, finding gratis iced-water, biscuits, and cheese.

"Well, Doctor," said I, "when shall we start?"

"At six o'clock this evening."

"Shall we take the Hudson railroad?"

"No; the *St. John*; a wonderful steamer, another world-a *Great Eastern* of the river, one of those admirable locomotive engines which go along with a will. I should have preferred showing you the Hudson by daylight, but the *St. John* only goes at night. Tomorrow, at five o'clock in the morning, we shall be at Albany. At six o'clock we shall take the New York Central Railroad, and in the evening we shall sup at Niagara Falls."

I did not discuss the Doctor's programme, but accepted it willingly.

The hotel lift hoisted us to our rooms, and some minutes later we descended with our tourist knapsacks. A fly took us in a quarter of an hour to the pier on the Hudson, before which was the *St. John*, the chimneys of which were already crowned with wreaths' of smoke.

CHAPTER XXXVI

The *St. John*, and its sister ship, the *Dean Richmond*, are two of the finest steam-ships on the river. They are buildings rather than boats; terraces rise one above another, with galleries and verandas. One would almost have thought it was a gardener's floating plantation. There are twenty flag-staffs, fastened with iron tressings, which consolidate the whole building. The two enormous paddleboxes are painted *al fresco,* like the tympans in the Church of St. Mark, at Venice. Behind each wheel rises the chimney of the two boilers, the latter placed outside, instead of in the hull of the steam- hip, a good precaution in case of explosion. In the center, between the paddles, is the machinery, which is very simple, consisting only of a single cylinder, a piston worked by a long cross-beam, which rises and falls like the monstrous hammer of a forge, and a single crank, communicating the movement to the axles of the massive wheels.

Passengers were already crowding on to the deck of the *St John*. Dean Pitferge and I went to secure a cabin; we got one which opened into an immense saloon, a kind of gallery with a vaulted ceiling, supported by a succession of Corinthian pillars. Comfort and luxury everywhere, carpets, sofas, ottomans, paintings, mirrors, even gas, made in a small gasometer on board.

At this moment the gigantic engine trembled and began to work. I went on to the upper terraces. At the stern was a gaily painted house, which was the steersman's room, where four strong men stood at the spokes of the double rudder-wheel. After walking about for a few minutes, I went down on to the deck, between the already heated boilers, from which light blue flames were issuing. Of the Hudson I could see nothing. Night came, and with it a fog thick enough to be cut The *St. John* snorted in the gloom like a true mastodon; we could hardly catch a glimpse of the lights of the towns scattered along the banks of the river, or the lanterns of ships ascending the dark water with shrill whistles.

At eight o'clock I went into the saloon. The Doctor took me to have supper at a magnificent restaurant placed between the decks, where we were served by an army of black waiters. Dean Pitferge informed me that the number of passengers on board was more than four thousand, reckoning fifteen-hundred emmigrants stowed away in the lower part of the steam-ship. Supper finished, we retired to our comfortable cabin.

At eleven o'clock I was aroused by a slight shock. The *St John* had stopped. The captain, finding it impossible to proceed in the darkness, had given orders to heave-to, and the enormous boat, moored in the channel, slept tranquilly at anchor.

At four o'clock in the morning the *St. John* resumed her course. I got up and went out under one of the verandahs. The rain had ceased, the fog cleared off, the water appeared, then the shores; the right bank, dotted with green trees and ·shrubs, which gave it the appearance of a long cemetery; in the background rose high hills, closing in the horizon by a graceful line; the left bank, on the contrary, was flat and marshy.

Dr. Pitferge had just joined me under the verandah.

"Good morning, friend," said he, after having drawn a good breath of air; "do you know we shall not be at Albany in time to catch the train, thanks to that wretched fog. This will modify my programme."

"So much the worse, Doctor, for we must be economical with our time."

"Right; we may expect to reach Niagara Falls at night instead of in the evening. That is not my fault, but we must be resigned."

The *St. John*, in fact, did not moor off the Albany quay before eight o'clock. The train had left, so we were obliged to wait till half-past one. In consequence of this delay we were able to visit the curious old city, which forms the legislative center of the State of New York: the lower town, commercial and thickly populated, on the right bank of the Hudson, and the high town, with its brick houses, public buildings, and its very remarkable museum of fossils. One might almost have thought it a large quarter of New York transported to the side of this hill, up which it rises in the shape of an amphitheatre.

At one o'clock, after having breakfasted, we went to the station, which was without any barrier or officials. The train simply stopped in the middle of the street, like an omnibus; one could get up and down at pleasure. The cars communicate with each other by bridges, which allow the traveler to go from one end of the train to the other. At the appointed time, without seeing either a guard or a porter, without a bell, without any warning, the brisk locomotive, a real gem of workmanship, started, and we were whirled away at the speed of fifty miles an hour. But instead of being boxed up, as one is in European trains, we were at liberty to walk about, buy newspapers and books, without waiting for stations. Refreshment buffets, bookstalls, everything was at hand for the traveler We were now crossing fields without fences, and forests newly cleared, at the risk of a collision with the felled trees; through new towns, seamed with rails, but still wanting in houses; through cities adorned with the most poetic names of ancient literature-Rome, Syracuse, and Palmyra. It was thus the Mohawk Valley, the land of Fenimore, which belongs to the American novelist, as does the land of Rob Roy to Walter Scott, glided before our eyes. For a moment Lake Ontario, which Cooper has made the scene of action of his master-work, sparkled on the horizon. All this theatre of the grand epopee of Leather Stocking, formerly a savage country, is now a civilized land. The Doctor did not appreciate the change, for he persisted in calling me Hawk's Eye, and would only answer to the name of Chingachgook.

At eleven o'clock at night we changed trains at Rochester; the spray from the Tennessee cascades fell over the cars in showers. At two o'clock in the morning, after having kept alongside the Niagara for several leagues without seeing it, we arrived at the village of Niagara Falls, and the Doctor conducted me to a magnificent hotel grandly named " Cataract House."

CHAPTER XXXVII

The Niagara is not a stream, not even a river; it is simply a weir sluice, a canal thirty-six miles long, which empties the waters of the Lakes Superior, Michigan, Huron, and Erie into the Ontario. The difference in the level of these last two lakes is three hundred and forty feet; this difference uniformly proportioned the whole of the width would hardly have created a "rapid; " but the Falls alone absorb half the difference in level, whence their formidable power.

This Niagarine trench separates the United States from Canada. Its right bank is American and its left English; on one side policemen, on the other not the shadow of one.

On the morning of the 12th of April, at break of day, the Doctor and I walked down the wide street of Niagara Falls, which is the name of the village situated on the banks of the Falls. It is a kind of small watering-place, three hundred miles from Albany, built in a healthy and charming situation, provided with sumptuous hotels and comfortable villas, which the Yankees and Canadians frequent in the season. The weather was magnificent, the sun warmed the cold atmosphere, a dull, distant roar was heard, and I saw vapours on the horizon which could not be clouds.

"Is that the Fall?" I asked of the Doctor.

"Patience!" replied Pitferge.

In a few minutes we were on the banks of the Niagara. The river was flowing peacefully along; it was clear, and not deep, with numerous projections of grey rock emerging here and there. The roar of the cataract grew louder and: louder, but as yet we could not see it. A wooden bridge, supported by iron arches, united the left bank to an island in the midst of the current; on to this bridge the Doctor led me. Above, stretched the river as far as the eye could reach; down the stream, that is to say on our right, the first unevenness of a rapid was noticeable; then, at half a mile from the bridge, the earth suddenly gave- way, and clouds of spray filled the air. This was the American fall, which we could not see. Beyond, on the Canadian side, lay a peaceful country, with hills, villas, and bare trees.

"Don't look! Don't look!" cried the Doctor to me; "reserve yourself, shut your eyes, and do not open them until I tell you!"

I hardly listened to my original, but continued to look. The bridge crossed, we set foot on the island known as Goat Island. It is a piece of land of about seventy acres, covered with trees, and intersected with lovely avenues with carriage drives. It is like a bouquet thrown between the American and Canadian Falls, separated from the shore by a distance of three hundred yards. We ran under the great trees, climbed the slopes, and went down the steps; the thundering roar of the falls was redoubled, and the air saturated with spray.

"Look!" cried the Doctor.

Coming from behind a mass of rock, the Niagara appeared in all its splendour. At this spot it meets with a sharp angle of land, and falling round it, forms the Canadian cascade, called the "Horse-Shoe Fall," which falls from a height of one hundred and fifty-eight feet, and is two miles broad.

In this, one of the most beautiful spots in the world, Nature has combined everything to astonish the eye. The fall of the Niagara singularly favours the effects of light and shade; the sunbeams falling on the water, capriciously diversify the colour; and those who have seen this effect, must admit that it is without paralleL In fact, near Goat Island the foam is white; it is then a fall of snow, or a heap of melted silver, pouring into the abyss. In the center of the cataract the colour of the water is a most beautiful sea-green, which indicates its depth, so that the *Detroit*, a ship drawing twenty feet and launched on the current, was able to descend the falls without grazing.

Towards the Canadian shore the whirlpool, on the contrary, looks like metal shining beneath the luminous rays, and it is melted gold which is now poured into the gulf. Below, the river is invisible from the vapours which rise over it. I caught glimpses, however, of- enormous blocks of ice accumulated by the cold of winter; they take the form of monsters, which, with open jaws, hourly absorb the hundred millions of tons poured into them by the inexhaustible Niagara. Half a mile below the cataract the river again became tranquil, and presented a smooth surface, which the winds of April had not yet been able to ruffle.

"And now for the middle of the torrent," said the Doctor to me.

I could not imagine what the Doctor meant by those words, until he pointed to a tower built on the edge of a rock some hundred feet from the shore, almost overhanging the precipice. This monument, raised in 1833, by a certain audacious being, one Judge Porter, is called the "Terrapin Tower."

We went down the steps of Goat Island, and, coming to the height of the upper course of the Niagara, I saw a bridge, or rather some planks, thrown from one rock to the other, which united the tower with the banks of the river.

The bridge was but a few feet from the abyss, and below it roared the torrent. We ventured on these planks, and in a few minutes reached the rock which supported Terrapin Tower. This round tower, forty-five feet in height, is built of stone, with a circular balcony at its summit, and a roof covered with red stucco. The winding staircase, on which thousands of names are cut, is wooden. Once at the top of the tower, there is nothing to do but cling to the balcony and look.

The tower is in the midst of the cataract. From its summit the eye plunges into the depths of the abyss, and peers into the very jaws of the ice monsters, as they swallow the torrent. One feels the rock tremble which supports it. It is impossible to hear anything but the roaring of the surging water. The spray rises to the top of the monument, and splendid rainbows are formed by the sun shining on the vapourized water.

By a simple optical illusion, the tower seems to move with a frightful rapidity, but, happily, in the opposite direction to the fall, for, with the contrary illusion, it would be impossible to look at the gulf from giddiness.

Breathless and shivering, we went for a moment inside the top landing of the tower, and it was then that the Doctor took the opportunity of saying to me,- "This Terrapin Tower, my dear sir, will some day fall into the abyss, and perhaps sooner than is expected."

“Ah! Indeed!"

"There is no doubt about it. The great Canadian Fall recedes insensibly, but still, it recedes. The tower, when it was first built in 1833, was much farther from the cataract. Geologists say that the fall, in the space of thirty-five thousand years, will be found at Queenstown, seven miles up the stream. According to Mr. Bakewell, it recedes a yard in a year; but according to Sir Charles Lyell one foot only. The time will come when the rock which supports the tower, worn away by the water, will glide down the Falls of the cataract. Well, my dear sir, remember this: the day when the Terrapin Tower falls, there will be some eccentrics who will descend the Niagara with it."

I looked at the Doctor, as if to ask him if he would be of that number, but he signed for me to follow him, and we went out again to look at the "Horse-Shoe Fall," and the surrounding country. We could now distinguish the American Fall, slightly curtailed and separated by a projection of the island, where there is another small central cataract one hundred feet wide; the American cascade, equally fine, falls perpendicularly. Its height is one hundred and sixty-four feet. But in order to have a good view of it it is necessary to stand facing it, on the Canadian side.

All day we wandered on the banks of the Niagara, irresistibly drawn back to the tower, where the roar of the water, the spray, the sunlight playing on the vapours, the excitement, and the briny odour of the cataract, holds you in a perpetual ecstasy. Then we went back to Goat Island, to get the Fall from every point of view, without ever being wearied of looking at it. The Doctor would have taken me to see the " Grotto of Winds," hollowed out underneath the central Fall, but access to it was not allowed, on account of the frequent falling away of the rocks.

At five o'clock we went back to the hotel, and after a hasty dinner, served in the American fashion, we returned to Goat Island. The Doctor wished to go and see the "Three Sisters," charming little islets scattered at the head of the island; then, with the return of evening, he led me back to the tottering rock of Terrapin Tower. The last rays of the setting sun had disappeared behind the grey hills, and the moon shed her soft clear light over the landscape. The shadow of the tower stretched across the abyss; farther down the stream the water glided silently along, crowned with a light mist. The Canadian shore, already plunged in darkness, contrasted vividly with the moon-lit banks of Goat Island, and the village of Niagara Falls. Below us, the gulf, magnified by the uncertain light, looked like a bottomless abyss, in which roared the formidable torrent. What effect! What artist could ever depict such a scene, either with the pen or paint-brush? For some minutes a moving light appeared on the horizon; it was the signal light of a train crossing the Niagara bridge at a distance of two miles from us. Here we remained silent and motionless on the top of the tower until midnight, leaning over the waters which possessed such a fascination. Once, when the moon-beams caught the liquid dust at a certain angle, I had a glimpse of a milky band of transparent ribbon trembling in the shadows. It was a lunar rainbow, a pale irradiation of the queen of the night, whose soft light was refracted through the mist of the cataract.

CHAPTER XXXVIII

The next day, the 13th of April, the Doctor's programme announced a visit to the Canadian shore. We had only to follow the heights of the bank of the Niagara for two miles to reach the suspension bridge. We started at seven o'clock in the morning. From the winding path on the right bank we could see the tranquil waters of the river, which no longer felt the perturbation of its fall.

At half-past seven we reached the suspension bridge. It is the bridge, on which the Great Western and New York Central Railroads meet, and the only one which gives access to Canada on the confines of the State of New York. This suspension bridge is formed of two platforms; the upper one for trains, and the lower for carriages and pedestrians. Imagination seems to lose itself in contemplating this stupendous work. This viaduct, over which trains can pass, suspended at a height of two hundred and fifty feet above the Niagara, again transformed into a rapid at this spot. This suspension bridge, built by John A. Roebling, of Trenton, New Jersey, is eight hundred feet long, and twenty-four wide; the iron props fastened to the shore prevent it from swinging; the chains which support it, formed of four thousand wires, are ten inches in diameter, and can bear a weight of twelve thousand four hundred tons. The bridge itself weighs but eight hundred tons, and cost five hundred thousand dollars. Just as we reached the center a train passed over our heads, and we felt the platform bend under its weight.

It is a little below this bridge that Blondin crossed the Niagara, on a rope stretched from one shore to the other, and not, as is generally supposed, across the falls. However, the undertaking was none the less perilous; but if Blondin astonished us by his daring, what must we think of his friend who accompanied him, riding on his back during this aerial promenade ?

"Perhaps he was a glutton," said the Doctor, "and Blondin made wonderful omelets on his tight-rope."

We were now on Canadian ground, and we walked up the left bank of the Niagara, in order to see the Falls under a new aspect Half an hour later we reached the English hotel, where the Doctor ordered our breakfast, whilst I glanced through the "Travellers' Book," where figured several thousand names: among the most celebrated I noticed the following :Robert Peel, Lady Franklin, Comte de Paris, Due de Chartres, Prince de Joinville, Louis Napoleon (1846), Prince and Princess Napoleon, Barnum (with his address), Maurice Sand (†865), Agassis (1854), Almonte, Prince Hohenlohe, Rothschild, Bertin (Paris), Lady Elgin, ·Burkhardt (1832), &c.

"And now let us go under the Falls," said the Doctor to me, when we had finished breakfast.

I followed Dean Pitferge. A negro conducted us to the dressing-room, where we were provided with waterproof trousers, macintoshes, and glazed hats. Thus equipped, our guide led us down a slippery path, obstructed by sharp edged stones, to the lower level of the Niagara. Then we passed behind the great fall through clouds of spray, the cataract falling before us like the curtain of a theatre before the actors. But what a theatre! Soaked, blinded, deafened, we could neither see nor hear in this cavern as hermetically closed by the liquid sheets of the cataract as though Nature had sealed it in by a wall of granite.

At nine o'clock we returned to the hotel, where they relieved us of our streaming clothes. Going back again to the bank, I uttered a cry of surprise and joy,-

"Captain Corsican!"

The Captain heard, and came towards me.

"You here!" he cried; "what a pleasure to see you again!"

"And Fabian? And Ellen?" I asked, shaking both his hands.

"They are here, and going on as well as possible; Fabian full of hope, almost merry; and our poor Ellen little by little regaining reason."

"But how is it that I meet you at the Niagara?"

"The Niagara," repeated Corsican. "Well, it is the principal resort of English and Americans in the warm months. They come here to breathe, to be cured by the sublime spectacle of the Falls. Our Ellen seemed to be struck at first sight by this glorious scenery, and we have come to stay on the banks of the Niagara. You see that villa, 'Clifton House,' in the midst of those trees, half way up the hill; that is where we all live, with Mrs. R-, Fabian's sister, who is devoted to our poor friend."

"Has Ellen recognized Fabian ?" I asked.

"No, not yet," replied the Captain. "You are aware, however, that at the moment when Drake was struck dead, Ellen had a brief interval of consciousness. Her reason became clear in the gloom which surrounded her, but this did not last long. At the same time, since we brought her to breathe this fresh air in this quiet place, the doctor has discovered a sensible improvement in her condition. She is calm, her sleep is tranquil, but there is a look in her eyes as though she were trying to think of something past or present."

"Ah," my dear friend!" cried I, "you will cure her; but where are Fabian and his betrothed?"

"Look!" said Corsican, and he pointed towards the shore of the Niagara.

In the direction indicated by the Captain I saw Fabian, who had not yet noticed us. He was standing on a rock, and a few feet in front of him sat Ellen perfectly motionless, Fabian watching her all the time. This spot on the left bank is known by the name of "Table Rock." It is a kind of rocky promontory jutting out into the river, which roars at a distance of four hundred feet below. Formerly it was more extensive, but the crumbling away of large pieces of rock has now reduced it to a surface a few yards square.

Ellen seemed absorbed in speechless ecstasy. From this place the aspect of the Falls is "most sublime," as say the guides, and they are right. It gives a view of two cataracts; on the right the " Canadian Fall," the crest of which, crowned with vapours, shuts in the horizon an one side, like the horizon of the sea. In front is the "American Fall," and above, the elegant village of Niagara Falls, half hidden in the trees; on the left, the whole perspective of the river flowing rapidly between its high banks, and below the torrent struggling against the overthrown icebergs.

Corsican, the Doctor, and I went towards Table Rock, but I did not want to disturb Fabian. Ellen was as motionless as a statue. What impression was this scene making on her mind? Was reason gradually coming back to her under the influence of the grand spectacle? Suddenly I saw Fabian step towards her. Ellen had risen quickly, and was going near to the abyss, with her arms extended towards the gulf; but all at once she stopped, and passed her hand rapidly across her forehead, as if she would drive away some thought. Fabian, pale as death, but self-possessed, with one bound placed himself between Ellen and the chasm; the latter shook back her fair hair, and her graceful figure staggered. Did she see Fabian? No. One would have said it was a dead person coming back to being, and looking round for life!

Captain Corsican and I dared not move, although, being so near the abyss, we dreaded some catastrophe; but the Doctor kept us back.

"Let Fabian alone," said he.

I heard the sobs which escaped from the young woman's heaving breast, the inarticulate words which came from her lips; she seemed as though she were trying to speak, but could not. At last she uttered these words :

"My God! My God! Where am I, Where am I?"

"She was conscious that some one was near her, for she half turned round, and her whole face seemed transfigured. There was a new light in her eyes, as she saw Fabian, trembling and speechless, standing before her with outstretched arms.

" Fabian! Fabian! " cried she, at last.

Fabian caught her in his arms, where she fell in an unconscious state. He uttered a piercing cry, thinking that Ellen was dead, but the Doctor interposed.

"Don't be alarmed," said he; "this crisis, on the contrary, will be the means of saving her!"

Ellen was carried to Clifton House and put to bed, where she recovered consciousness and slept peacefully. Fabian, encouraged by the Doctor, was full of hope. Ellen had recognized him! Coming back to us, he said to me,-

"We shall save her, we shall save her! Every day! Watch her coming back to life. Today, tomorrow, perhaps she will be restored to me. Ah! The just God be praised! We will stay here as long as it is necessary for her, shall we not, Archibald?"

The Captain clasped Fabian in his arms; then the latter turned to the Doctor and me. He loaded us with thanks, and inspired us with the hope which filled his breast, and never was there better reason for hope-Ellen's recovery was near at hand.

But we must be starting, and there was hardly an hour for us to reach Niagara Falls. Ellen was still sleeping when we left our dear friends. Fabian and Corsican bid us a last farewell, after having promised we should have news of Ellen by telegraph, and at noon we left Clifton House.

CHAPTER XXXIX

Some minutes later we were descending a long flight of steps on the Canadian side, which led to the banks of the river, covered with huge sheets of ice. Here a boat was waiting to take us to "America." One passenger had already taken his place in it. He was an engineer from Kentucky, and acquainted the Doctor with his name and profession. We embarked without loss of time, and by dint of steering, so as to avoid the blocks of ice, reached the middle of the river, where the current offered a clear passage.

From here we had a last view of the magnificent Niagara cataract. Our companion observed it with a thoughtful air.

"Is it not grand, sir? Is it not magnificent?" said I to him.

"Yes," replied he; "but what a waste of mechanical force, and what a mill might be turned with such a fall as that!"

Never did I feel more inclined to pitch an engineer into the water! On the other bank a small and almost vertical railroad, worked by a rope on the American side, hoisted us to the top. At half-past one we took the express, which put us down at Buffalo at a quarter past two. After visiting this large new town, and tasting the water of Lake Erie, we again took the New York Central Railway at six o'clock in the evening. The next day, on leaving the comfortable beds of a "sleeping car," we found ourselves at Albany and the Hudson Railroad, which runs along the left bank of the river, brought us to New York a few hours later.

The next day, the 15th of April, in company with the indefatigable Doctor, I went over the city, East River, and Brooklyn. In the evening I bade farewell to the good Dean Pitferge, and I felt, in leaving him, that I left a friend.

Tuesday, the 16th of April, was the day fixed for the departure for the *Great Eastern*. At eleven o'clock I went to Thirty-seventh pier, where the tender was to await the passengers. It was already filled with people and luggage when I embarked. Just as the tender was leaving the quay some one caught hold of my arm, and turning round I saw Dr. Pitferge.

"You!" I cried; "and are you going back to Europe?"

"Yes, my dear sir."

"By the *Great Eastern*?"

“Undoubtedly," replied the amiable original, smiling; "I have considered the matter, and have come to the conclusion that I must go. Only think, this may be the *Great Eastern's last voyage, the one which she will never complete."*

The bell for departure had rung, when one of the waiters from Fifth Avenue Hotel came running up to me, and put a telegram into my hands, dated from Niagara Falls: Ellen has awakened; her reason has entirely returned to her," said Captain Corsican, " and the doctor has every hope of her recovery."

I communicated this good news to Dean Pitferge.

“Every hope for her indeed! Every hope!" said my fellow traveler, in a sarcastic tone. "I also have every hope for her, but what good does that do? Any one may have great hopes for you, for me, for all of us, but at the same time he may be just as much wrong as right."

Twelve days later we reached Brest, and the day following Paris. The return passage was made without any misfortune, to the great displeasure of Dean Pitferge, who always expected to see the great ship wrecked. And now, when I am sitting at my own table, if I had not my daily notes before me, I should think that the *Great Eastern*, that floating city in which I lived for a month, the meeting of Ellen and Fabian, the peerless Niagara, all these were the visions of a dream. Ah! How delightful is traveling, "even when one does return," in spite of what the Doctor may say to the contrary.

For eight months I heard nothing of my original, but one day the post brought me a letter, covered with many coloured stamps, which began with these words :-

"On board the Corinquay, Auckland Rocks. At last we have been shipwrecked."

And ended thus :-

"Was never in better health. Very heartily yours,

DEAN PITFERGE."

The End

2576334R10070

Printed in Great Britain
by Amazon.co.uk, Ltd.,
Marston Gate.